# Message to the
# Nurse of
# Dreams

# Message to the
# Nurse of
# Dreams

a collection of short fiction by

## Lisa Sandlin

### Cinco
### Puntos
### Press

## Acknowledgments

Some of these stories have appeared in the following publications: "Vidor" appeared in *Southwest Review* and "If You Don't Watch Out" appeared in *Crazy Horse*.

Library of Congress Cataloging-in-Publication Data

Sandlin, Lisa.
    Message to the nurse of dreams: a collection of short fiction / by Lisa Sandlin.
        p.   cm. — (Hell yes! Texas women series)
      ISBN 0-938317-27-X
      I. Title. II. Series : Hell yes! Texas women series.
PS3569.A5168M4    1997
813'.54—dc21

                          97-343
                          CIP

This book is funded in part by the generous support of the Texas Commission on the Arts

Lisa Sandlin would like to thank the National Endowment for the Arts for their support; and the Texas Institute of Letters and The University of Texas at Austin for awarding her the Dobie-Paisano Fellowship which provided her with the time and space to complete this book.

Cover image "Yes" © 1990 by Keith Carter from his book *MOJO*.
Photograph of Lisa Sandlin © 1995 by Jane Grossenbacher.
Cover and book design by Geronimo Garcia of El Paso, Texas.

# Contents

For Lee Sandlin and Evan Lee Briggs

# If You Don't Watch Out

DAD TORE US away from the car radio—they were playing the Beatles' new one, "Ticket to Ride"—and herded us in, Bill bitching under his breath the whole way. The dining room was almost full. People crossed the carpeted floor with plates from the buffet, waitresses splayed out tray tables, busboys rattled carts of dirty dishes. It was Labor Day Sunday at the Holiday Inn, which was why the restaurant was busy and my brother was beside himself—he foresaw maximum humiliation potential. Poor Dad, he always hoped he could snap Mom out of it with a treat, like this lunch, or a drive to the beach with Van Cliburn on the eight-track. Bill and I had a trickier relationship with hope.

We hit the buffet table, loaded our plates wth mashed potatoes and desserts and dove back into the booth to let Dad go. Mom slid out of her seat and waited for him, kneading her hands. Some people turned our way; Bill squirmed, and tapped her arm. When Dad returned with two plates, he let her sit on the outside, a mistake I would not have made. Mom stared down at the ham and buttered roll and mauve congealed salad. Her flat cheeks puffed but she caught herself and swallowed.

Bill's spit sprayed my ear. "The principle of claustropho-bia as applied to time," he whispered bitterly, meaning we were in for a long and horrible lunch.

But then—a Negro family came in.

They waited by the hostess stand, by the large This Es-tablishment Reserves the Right to Refuse Service sign. A man at the table next to our booth turned the airy red of a cooked crab. The hostess, with a handful of menus, backed up into an office; the manager hustled out and seated the family at a corner table by the swinging kitchen door. After only a minute in those seats, they got up and moved to a table directly in the center of the dining room.

"I'll be damned," Dad said, in wonder. "Right here. Right here in Port Sabine."

"Get real, Dad. This is 1965." Bill's mood had transformed into brightness. He got up on his knees to see better.

The father of the family pulled out the mother's chair. His white cuffs and close-to-the-skull hair gleamed. He moved as though the soles of his shoes were waxed—graceful quar-ter turn, sliding out the chair, hint of swivel, tucking the mother into her place. The beautiful mother wore a green pillbox hat. A deep gold sublayer glowing through her skin tinged her face, her almond eyes with sweetness.

The daughter was about my age, fifteen, what people call a Big Girl. Like me. She wore a pink dress with a bell skirt, her breasts distributed throughout the whole bodice section. Her jaggy black hair was slicked back and held down with a pink stretch bandeau.

Dad said, "I know damn well what year it is," then low-ered his voice. "You thought that one of these old boys in here just might be armed?"

"They *know* that," I said.

The girl's eyes were the opaque black of igneous rock and her jaw was set like a gar's. Her brother looked like a cute little walking dead boy they'd got out of a funeral home be-fore the eyes could be sewed shut.

Waitresses and busboys began to line the walls, to watch. At a few tables people kept eating. Bill hadn't been so interested in anything except "The Lake Regions of Central Africa" (he worshipped Sir Richard Burton) for about three years. He gestured in Mom's direction—she weighed maybe ninety again—wiped his forehead and pretended to flick the sweat off, grinning at me. We stared at the Negro family, who had folded their menus. Nobody was watching Mom.

She floated up like an unattended balloon and drifted across the dining room to the grand piano in the far corner. Mom sat at the bench and shrugged off the straps of her sundress, which put the top of it in danger of gravity. She blew on her fingers.

Eyes wide, I nudged Bill. His voice cracked as it hadn't done for a couple of years. "Jesus, Dad." Bill threw down his fork. "Annie," Dad half rose, losing the napkin on his lap. Mom's fingers were sinking to the keys.

The Negro family pushed back their chairs. They'd chosen the buffet, which gave them a chance to rise again, cross the room, fill their plates, walk back across the room and sit down. That also let them be sure nobody in the kitchen did anything ugly to their food. The father smiled slightly. They looked at no one.

Bent over the piano in her descending sundress, Mom played "Exodus." The family ate and drank to her faint piano. Bill was wedged down in the booth, sitting on his kidneys; Dad had pointed himself outward, toward Mom, his elbows weighting his knees. It was like watching a silent movie in which the actors carry suitcases and one of the suitcases has a trip-wire bomb, but you don't know which one.

Finally the family laid down their napkins. The manager appeared as though shot from a trap door to take their money. The smiling father's white-cuffed wrist made a tiny fillip as he dropped a dollar on the table. He held the door for the children, and then for his pretty wife. While the whole restaurant charted the family's exit, Dad rushed the piano.

"My amazing Annie," he said when he had Mom at our booth again. "That is some natural talent. Isn't it, Mayda?" I nodded. Dad's tone was fakey but he was right. Mom had never had a lesson in her life; something unique in her brain just told her how to play. He wrapped her hand around a fork. We all watched the fork leave her fingers. He jerked his eyebrows, meaning we should encourage her.

"What do you want, man?" Bill jumped up, and jammed his hands in his pockets. Before he ran off, he said Mom looked like the cat when it had distemper—she couldn't hold her head up over her water dish. I tried to hug Mom but it didn't take, so I followed Bill.

In dreams sometimes, being chased toward crumbley cliffs, I could at the very last second shoot up safe into the air. This wasn't flying; more a pure propulsion for my life's sake. Bill believed we'd been rescued when we really hadn't but maybe that was what had been happening for the Negro family—a pure propulsion for the sake of their whole lives. I scanned the parking lot for them but they were gone forever.


BUT THEY WEREN'T, exactly. On Tuesday, our first day of school, the girl from the Holiday Inn was escorted into science. Mr. Buddy Johnson, the principal, introduced Geneece Paylette to us, and then loitered around in the hall. Geneece Paylette's thin socks were rolled down into rings on her ankles. The thirty of us in Miss Baxter's Life Science watched her sit down, open her notebook, and take out a yellow pencil. The minute she looked up, we turned around. The teacher was starting.

Miss Baxter prowled the aisles, warning us cheating reaped its own reward. Her heavy black eyebrows, slightly bugged eyes and bulb nose were larger than normal: Miss Baxter could be seen clearly from far away, the way a jack o'lantern can be seen from the street. When she was in college, she said, she allowed a boy, a football player, to copy her test. The professor called them both up to his lectern and gave the boy his paper back with an F on it. Then he dropped Miss Baxter's test on the floor so that, in front of all her classmates, she had to stoop all the way down and pick it up. Her popped eyes dared us to guess: Her test had an F on it, too. And the football player never spoke to her after that.

Cheaters reap their own reward, she said again, knocking her knuckles on the Negro girl's desk. We twisted around in our seats to watch Miss Baxter's huge face glowering above Geneece Paylette's head. Did her speech just happen there? Or did she mean something?

By Friday, we knew. She took roll and Geneece Paylette was absent. Then Miss Baxter didn't talk about molecules or mitosis. She went up and down the desk rows talking about Niggers. She said they would get away with anything they could; that was their proven nature. They would cheat, they would steal, they would get on welfare and never work; laziness was a genetic fact of their blood. Miss Baxter said Geneece Paylette for all her Supreme Court federal integration and her NAACP was just a Garden-Variety Nigger.

The class shifted in their seats; I drew fast spirals on my paper. Should I hate Geneece Paylette because she was colored, or rather, Negro? What I knew of her, I admired. The Holiday Inn in the company of your family was one thing, but busting the ninth grade of Port Sabine High School all by yourself was another. All of a sudden the shifting and the foot shuffling stopped. I looked up.

Geneece Paylette stepped through the doorway, books tight against her chest and a tardy slip in her hand. Her lips were pressed together. She set her tennis shoes down so deliberately her footfalls made no sound. When she was settled, she knocked the pink tardy slip—Miss Baxter would have to bend way, way down to get it—off her desk and let it flutter to the floor.

Bill hiked up on one elbow to listen to the story. "That's

the girl in the restaurant?" he asked. He was in bed all covered up, with some Dr. Peppers, and five library books with ragged foldout maps, and the air conditioner blasting.

"Same one."

He said, "Subtle. I bet those assholes didn't even get what she was doing. What about Miss Bastard?"

"Oh, she got it." Miss Baxter looked like they'd exhumed her and opened the coffin on her rigor-mortis face.

Bill grinned. But then I asked him where Mom and Dad were, and he turned against me.

He said I outweighed him and the only reason a guy would ever ask me out would be to squeeze my tits. He said I was the stupidest quasi-human extant in the mid-twentieth century. If I didn't know where Mom and Dad were. If I didn't know that. By goddamn now.

That meant Mom was back in Hotel Dieu, the Catholic hospital with the special ward. The place was submarine gray, full of indigents, crazy people, Pine Sol, and nuns. Mom would be hooked up to a thousand volts, with a stick between her teeth so she didn't bite off her tongue. Dad was probably hunched over in the dim lobby with a clipboard on his knees. I ran out of Bill's room, but he and the blanket dragged after me. "Mayda!"

I didn't read like my brother but I had a theory that people went around showing by every word and by everything they did, what they were. Miss Baxter was ugly and cruel. Mom was crazy. Bill was scared he was, too. I wanted to be more like Geneece Paylette—she had dignity; she had a snap-fish jaw. I informed Bill, "I'm going to my job now." But when he said Mr. Baxevanis probably wanted to squeeze my tits too, I punched him. Bill retracted inside the blanket, and I left him all humped over.


ON THE WAY down the street, I blocked out Bill's meanness and tried instead to guess how Mr. Baxevanis and I might fix the house when I got there. I did remind myself to knock three times. He had to be careful: Mr. Baxevanis's blood sister was Miss Baxter. Their mother had died and left her house with the live oaks to him, the son from New York, while willing the other two children—Miss Baxter and a brother, Pete—a mother's eternal love. Now those two were at war with my employer.

Mr. Baxevanis was short like his sister but older, the skin at both eyes crosshatched with lines like little fish nets. His swept-back hair shone a bright burgundy color in the sunlight, especially around the temples. His new house—shared with a parrot named Josephine Baker—was wonderful. The house sat back from the street, protected by a curly wrought-iron gate and sheltered by two entwined live oaks with sinewy black trunks and ribs. Its shuttered windows rose high enough to stand in. The floors were built of wide polished planks as smooth and beautiful as honey; walking on them rattled the glass in the breakfronts and trembled the bare feet of Mr. Baxevanis's mother's ceramic shepherdesses. He said, "Mama knew my brother and sister would make their way." He told me this the first day I helped him—for seventy-five cents an hour, our arrangement—pack and unpack. "Me, she wasn't so sure." His big, rounded dark eyes moistened a little as he nested a figurine in tissue paper.

He was sad they blamed him but truly happy to have the house. "A place to be," he'd sighed deeply as he turned a circle. Mr. Baxevanis had me pack the shepherdesses away and fill the breakfronts with paper-jacketed books. He replaced his mother's squat mahogany furniture with puffy upholstery, wicker end tables, and a grand yellow vase we planted with peacock feathers.

I pounded three times and fidgeted on the welcome mat. "It's Mayda," I said, as soon as the door cracked and a round eye the color of a nice black olive scanned my face. Mr. Baxevanis closed the door quickly behind me. The rugs he'd ordered from New York had arrived, so we covered the centers of the pine floors with them, settling a new quiet on the house. "My God, no screams, no sirens, listen," he said, when we'd finished two rooms, and we could hear the crickets playing their peaceful evening song. We listened for a while. Then I helped him roll out the last rug, a green and azure universe. "This carpet looks like the Garden of Eden," I said. "With no people in it."

He cocked his head. I squished my breasts under my elbows. "All not hunkey dorey, May?" he asked.

"It's Mayda." He'd been getting my name wrong for three weeks.

"Well, May-da, you look old enough to drink coffee." He brought me a doll cup, and himself one just like it, on two doll saucers. I loved holding the tiny handle. "You do like lots of sugar?" he asked, and breathed *Good* when I nodded. We sat. We sipped. The crickets sang like a tide: loud then soft, forward then back; green evening slanted through the windows. After a while I sighed, too.


OUR SPEECH TEACHER Mr. Wafflert told us to write a dialogue on "America Our Country," and then to practice it with a classmate. Mr. Wafflert was good-natured and unspecifically foreign; no one knew how or why—except that Port Sabine's muddy ship channel met the ocean sea—he'd ended up here. We watched his mistake dawn on him.

Seeing amid all the pairs and one trio of students Geneece partnerless and stone-faced, he waded out into the desks, waving his red pencil. "Pum," Mr. Wafflert said, snapping his fingers as though he'd forgotten and slipped us the wrong assignment, silly him.

"First work is a pum, all to memorize and recite, next a dialogue. Choose from your English books or go to the library."

Sammy Forster slammed his books together and took out the door, followed by most of the boys. Smiling Liddy Rice didn't go. Her mother had trained her in recitations, and every Halloween she acted out a poem called "The Goblins Will Get You if You Don't Watch Out." Liddy was miniature and slight, like the drawing of a fairy. While she recited I used to study the scar on her pointed face, a long whitened slash by one ear, and imagine all the ways it could have settled there.

To remind Dad that the world was still going on, I asked him for a poem. Gradually, as though on a crane, his newspaper lowered. He started the last verse of "Casey at the Bat," the stuff about children playing somewhere and somewhere everyone else being happy. He trailed off, crimped a hand to hide his eyes, and started talking about Mom. Bill left the room; his door banged.

When I asked Mr. Baxevanis if he knew of any poems, he sat alert, caressing his throat. His brother Pete had been to see him the day before with a subpoena from a lawyer. He'd refused to let his brother in. Mr. Baxevanis spoke from the shutters, the brother yelled, until in a fit he had kicked his legs like a donkey and stalked away through the live oaks.

"Break the will! Break the will! He said it over so many times Josephine picked it up." Mr. Baxevanis wiped his eyes, fetched me two powdered-sugar crescent cookies on a plate, then darted to his shelves and pulled out a book. He set it on his knee and did not open it for some time. Then he let me, and I opened it, to a poem of love.

On the day I said it, Liddy sashayed her way through the Goblins. She asked to have the fan off. She started slow, pivoting to take in the range of us, and worked up to the familiar climax. "The goblins . . . Oh!" . . . she shook her finger. *Oh oh,* A.B. Jones cooed sourly, mincing his shoulders. "The goblins will get you—" Liddy widened yellow-brown eyes. "The goblins will get you if you don't watch out!" She dropped a curtsy at the finish. The class whistled and applauded; Mr. Wafflert smiled, index finger on his cheek.

Three of us were left: Sammy Forster, Geneece Paylette,

and me. Over the renewed whine of the electric fan, Sammy recited part of "The Rime of the Ancient Mariner." His body veered left, then back right, keeping time. Sammy tolled the poem in deadly rhythm, phrases falling like blows from a galleymaster's whip.

At length! did cross! an al-ba-tross!
Through! the fog! it came!

For the first five lines we rolled along with him. After that A.B. Jones's head hit his desk and the epidemic was on. Mr. Wafflert traveled the hot room swatting necks with a mimeograph-paper baton. Only stage fright kept me awake. I read and reread my poem of love.

When I'd stopped at that page Mr. Baxevanis had blown out a breath and clutched the center of his forehead. "Oh dead aim." He shook his head briskly, and took the book from me to pass on. But he did not pass on. Instead his lips trembled as he read over the poem. He held his chest as though his heart had swelled. He studied me. Then he put the book in my hands. "Try it. Don't rush."

The poem, all simple words except for one I didn't know, seemed strange—it used no rhymes. Its speaker recalled a meeting and a parting, in plain talk, as if he were calmly telling it to you. Which words let me know how sad he was? None of them. But I raised my face, full of regret. I practiced the poem with Mr. Baxevanis nodding his head in agony at each line end. "Wait, wait," he'd begged and run to toss a cloth over Josephine's cage so the bird would not interrupt.

I looked out at my audience. Except for pixie-faced Liddy, still keyed up from the goblins, only a few pairs of half-mast eyes met mine. I said the poem with dignity and wistfulness. Mr. Wafflert's eyelashes fluttered as though struck by a mild wind; his pale nose reddened. Pink palm on brown face, Geneece Paylette softly laughed *Ha*.

I hadn't even sat down when Mr. Wafflert called her name, and coughed, and made a mark in his stiff red-backed grade book. The laugh went out of Geneece's face; she rose, walked to the front, gripped one hand on the other and gazed over all our heads. Geneece fixed her eyes on a distant point, maybe Sammy's doomed ship so far to sea. With her first words, heads came up and sleepy eyes cut sideways. She said "Invictus" with no rhythm we could follow but with stops that made sense of it.

Black as the night that covers me, Black . . .

Her eyebrows and chin were lifted. Her shoulders leveled, the rolled-down socks on her ankles lined up. Her low throaty voice propelled words over our heads. *Black black black in your white faces*, she said, gazing toward the cold blue sea, or the future.

The electric fan made breath again. The bell rang, and Mr. Wafflert asked to see me and Geneece. Liddy Rice lingered in the doorway fingering her scar but he did not ask to see her. He told Geneece she should attend the speech competition in the declamation category. She clutched her books to her chest and dipped her head, acting shy. This did not fit in with how I now thought of her: as a lone, girl hero. I stood right behind her, breathing, calculating her hair to be the texture of cotton candy. Mr. Wafflert crooked his finger and said I could compete, too, with practice. Then he cleared his throat and asked me, "Where did you get that pum?" I told him from my neighbor who loved books and rugs.

"Do you know what "deviate" means?" I shook my head but it seemed he could not bear to tell me.

In the hall over the sound of slamming lockers, I said to Geneece, "You really did good."

She didn't turn her high head at first; she said in a close-up voice, unlike the formal way she spoke in class, "Means butt-fucker. Just like that science teacher." But then she did look at me, and with a sheen of curiosity in her black eyes.


THREE DAYS LATER, a scream ricocheted down the hall from industrial arts. An ambulance took George Simcox and his finger away. That afternoon four burrhead Ag boys held Byron Dittweiler down, and cut off his long blond hair. Still no one had spoken to Geneece except me, and my mother had not telephoned from the special ward at Hotel Dieu, the ward Bill called The Electric Institute. At some point, she would telephone sounding ecstatic, so awfully relieved to be cured, either heart-crushingly earnest or throwing out with furious good will little jokes on herself and the other patients. Silverware would clink in the background as I listened to her breathless plan to surround our yard with Chinese bamboo. The first time—until we saw what happened when the bliss wore off—all of us were happy, too.

I went straight to Mr. Baxevanis's that afternoon after school, picked up his grocery and pharmacy lists—he was devouring Tums like chocolates, he claimed—and walked back with two bags, kicking the sweetgum leaves.

I was mulling over his motive for letting me read the class a poem like that. Truly I did not believe he meant to get me in trouble. No, he'd set the poem in my hands; I savored that. Searching out "deviate" in Bill's dictionary had not helped. The first definition read *a turning aside from the prescribed course*. Those words struck me—determined, gentle, brave. Except that I didn't find her gentle—Mr. Baxevanis was gentle!—the phrase described Geneece herself. The dictionary's second definition fit with the one she had offered. I knew Mr. Baxevanis was different from me but I also knew there was an island of kindness where we met, a time-out from everything. That kindness was not only on his part, and I valued him for how he caused me to be.

I stopped outside the wrought-iron gate. A mailman, his bag bumping, was chasing my employer up his walk under the live oaks. Mr. Baxevanis had a safe lead but then bobbled the door knob. The mailman's hand, flapping a letter, shot out. When the knob gave, Mr. Baxevanis did a standing leap into the house, slamming the door behind him. I set the groceries down and waited for the thwarted mailman to drag his bag back down the walk.

Mr. Baxevanis let me inside where he paced the carpets. "I'll have to get a dog," he complained, squeezing his temples. Josephine chattered shrilly *Papa, Papa*. "Can you name one breed that's not repulsive? I hate their hypocrisy. Their huge tongues."

"Why didn't you want that letter?" I asked him. "Here's your Tums."

"No no, dear, the question is why did I go out for air? That was a process server, Mayda. Pete and Lydia sent him. Yesterday it was a phone repairman. When I told him the phone was fine, he actually said, 'Reckon I'll be the judge of that.' My God, is it worth it?" His round black eyes beseeched me. "I'm in Alcatraz."

That he didn't expect me to answer hurt my pride. The law was on his side; Pete and Lydia would have to give up, and then . . . he would never need to be vigilant again. Was it worth it? "Oh look," I reproached him. I held out my arms at the ceiling fan in its rhythm, at the snug spines of the books, the wine and blue islands edged round by golden wood, the tall old windows with worn rose cushions on the window seats. Outside the live oaks tinted the September evening green; the crickets were awake and tuning up. Mr. Baxevanis blew his nose and, with one side of his mouth, smiled.


THE PHONE CALL came; relief washed over me when in a dazzling voice Mom asked for her Billiam. "No way." Bill would not leave the bed. "Tell her to hold on, Dad'll be home."

The blanket climbed over his mouth. I saw that in the night his nose had grown larger and bony, and developed a hump on the bridge, like Dad's. I told Bill he was weird but not crazy and he should just get out of bed and walk around with the rest of us. His eyes squeezed shut, then open again, but he stayed where he was.

I said Bill was in the bathroom, you know, and just couldn't come out right now.

"Well, tell my Billiam that I'm weaving him such pretty shirts on the loom here. And Mayda—" her voice quavered.

I stalled. "That little loom?"

"It does just fine! Yes that one, and Mayda . . . Oh Mayda . . ."

Here it came. She tore my name apart with love. In between pauses for her to catch her breath, she told me she was so grateful Lord she was crushed down on her knees grateful to be well. To be restored. Human again. I couldn't know how beautiful, how sacred it felt not to be separate from everyone else. Not to be lost. Could I imagine? Just try to imagine?

I said I would try very hard.

That was holy, she went on, not to be separate, could she count on me to please see that, her baby, her precious precious Mayda?

"Yeah, Mom," I whispered.

"They want me to hang up now," my mother said. "But I'll weave you something, too."

Mom weaving, her eyes all earnest—I laid my forehead on my knees and cried. Hope for Mom was like a good little house to live in. Once she had hope, she could love us again. In the hope phase she conceived enormous projects to benefit members of our family, the bamboo for Dad who liked privacy, the shirts (it would never be one shirt, it would be many) for Bill. She never thought of a project to benefit herself.

I could see Mom in Hotel Dieu's craft therapy room, her shoulders striped with light from the barred windows, weaving cloth strips on the loom. She was probably round-cheeked now from all the sugared orange-juice conductant, and flushed rosy with manic hope, such hope; she probably looked good.

I TOLD MR. Baxevanis to forget the stupid speech competition, but he said over his dead body, and to take my tonic without complaining. So I wound up choosing another poem by the same Greek poet. "A battle, hmmm." With a suspicious wave of his red pencil, Mr. Wafflert approved it. My poem described an attack by enemy Romans on a walled Greek city. The speaker worried about a soldier friend guarding city gates, and also about treasures which could not be replaced. Scrolls, gold and amethyst jewelry, perfumed salves, a garden of blue flowers, these were all named and, dear as any of these, the strength of two hearts. That was how the speaker returned to the soldier, a proud young man with a dreamy face. Still, the treasures were buried, safe and deep, and wily blue flowers replanted on top of them.

"Okay she loved the soldier but she loved her scrolls too, so she buried them in the garden and stuck the flowers back on top?" I asked.

"She?" Mr. Baxevanis glanced up from a match flame. "Oh, I see. You mean the speaker. A passionate, but yes, rather a practical mind at work there."

"Dear as any of these . . . does that mean *dear* dear?"

"Yes, but not sweetie pie and happy birthday to you. It means rare and expensive. So expensive you can't buy it . . . though you go to the store many, many times." Mr. Baxevanis's black eyebrows quivered.

He sat across from me, smoking a cigarette, his eyes narrowed with listening. He had closed every shutter to darken the room and removed the shade from his prism lamp so the bulb shone raw in my face. He said he was simulating stage conditions, a la New York.

When I finished he brought his fingertips together under his chin and canted his head, worried. I needed weight, he said, but when I stared he flung up a palm and went on, gravity he meant and lightness and an idea of rhythm that included silence. In order to deliver this poem properly, I needed wisdom or marvelous good luck, or an influence.

What was I going to wear?

"Doesn't matter, I'll be behind a podium," I said.

"Head presentation only." He bit his thumb.

I slumped on his ottoman.

"Oh, have some posture!" he exclaimed. Then, jumping up—"Sorry, the isolation is getting to me"— he suggested I invite a classmate or two over to practice with me; he would coach us all. Girls! he amended; he didn't want any trouble. He sighed. Josephine flew onto his shoulder, and he asked the parrot, "What else do we have to do?"

I told him there was only one person I would ask but I couldn't.

"And why not?" Irritable again, he set his hands on his hips.

"She's colored. I mean, Negro."

He drew in his chin. "God save me from this culture!" he cried. "No, no, I refuse to think it of you, Mayda. I hope . . ." he shook his head, "no, I'm quite certain you mean that you will have to work hard to assure her she will not feel uncomfortable in my home when she visits. Isn't that what you mean?"

"Sort of."

He waited, hands on hips tightening.

"She hates your sister."

"Oh." He relaxed into his normal height. "Yes, well, doesn't everyone?"

I asked him was his sister ever . . . different.

"She was." Mr. Baxevanis sat down, urged Josephine onto his finger and shooed her into the air. "Years ago Lydia was all right."

"What happened to her?"

He shrugged. "I guess I'd have to say that Lydia soured, like milk. The process was slow but chemically complete." Suddenly his eyes shone with inspiration. "Wait wait wait. Mayda, I see it!"

He dashed from the room and came back with an aquamarine scarf. He shaped it around my face, twisting it under my chin. As he tucked the ends up in the back, *Seventeen* magazine flashed before me: teeny skirts, teeny thighs, wild hair. The scarf was like the ones Susan Hayward wore in sport cars, to keep her permanent from blowing.

"I wear this inside?" I asked him.

He rolled his eyes. "Think of it as a costume, Mayda. You are creating a mood, a picture, just as the poem is. Costumes enhance the truth. Now, here's the thing . . . you want to look like the woman at the well."

"What woman?"

"Any woman, that's the point," he said. "Biblical, pagan, who cares, the perennial woman. Never be cute, Mayda, that's not your ticket at all. You will never be cute."

My throat thickened at that, and more: I saw I'd got my job because I was unlikely to suggest trouble to anyone.

He noticed, but he didn't look sorry for hurting my feelings. His olive face looked as matter-of-fact as when I'd asked him wasn't it true the law was on his side, and he'd answered, "The law is a whore." Now he added that I didn't see it yet but I'd already got a woman's body, and sorrow in my face. Then, brisk, he reminded me to invite my friend.


I WOULDN'T HAVE blamed Geneece for chickening out, but she came, and not alone. I ran out to get the gate. An old woman in a red cardigan sweater pushed up to the elbows craned from the bus steps, shading her eyes at both of us. The old woman stayed on the bus when it left. I asked Geneece who that was.

"My grandmother. Always fraid something gone swoop down and eat me up." Geneece smiled.

I liked how she smiled—in a freer way than she ever did at school—and spoke her easy language to me. Maybe this whole thing would go all right. "All I remember about my grandmother is she stuck straight pins in her collar."

"Oh yeah, my grandmother she sew, too," Geneece said.

I clanged the gate shut behind us and we talked about how neither of us knew how to sew more than buttons. We were both jittery with energy over the fact here we were right up next to what we didn't understand but might. Geneece said her grandmother wouldn't hem her skirts short but she made other girls' whatever length they asked for. That reminded me. "Your mother sure is beautiful." I'd been saving up this compliment to say to her. "She looks like a model."

We'd just started up the walk, but Geneece stopped. "Where you see my mother?" All the friendliness squeezed from her face.

A buzz ran down the outsides of my arms. I spilled out how I was at the Holiday Inn the day she and her family came and ate the buffet and that my mother was the one playing the piano and I'd thought her mother was really beautiful. Perfect. Geneece still looked unfriendly. Was it supposed to have been a secret, that she'd been at the Holiday Inn? I found myself telling her my mother was locked up in Hotel Dieu and I dreaded them letting her out because we had to teach her all the neighbors' names again and what grades we were in but sometimes I was afraid they'd never let her out and I just meant Geneece was lucky to have a mother so pretty and nice. Young, too. My forehead throbbed.

Geneece said, "She young all right. Bout nine or ten years older than me. My daddy he's round twelve years older than me." Seeing my expression, she frowned and changed her speech. "I don't know if I should tell you this."

"What?"

She backed up into the shadow of a live oak branch.

"Okay don't tell me," I said. "Forget about it." Such dead quiet under the live oaks, the crickets asleep in the four o'clock shade. No cars passed and no children shouted. We just stood there, sweaty and distrustful.

Geneece asked, "Your mama crazy?"

I wished I hadn't asked her for the practice because being

with her took so much effort I was tired already. "For all intents and purposes," I said.

She nodded in a calm way. Watching slant-eyed for my reaction, she told me how the family had been assembled, a combination of invitees and volunteers. Cannon, the father, organized. Geneece volunteered and she got Vincent, the brother, to say he'd do it, too, though later he wanted to back out. Vincent lived down the street from her. Sheela, that was the mother, was an invitee. The organizers went to her house, convinced her she was too pretty and too soft for anyone to want to hurt.

I blurted, "Don't you ever think you're like a hero?"

Geneece screwed up her eyes and wrinkled her nose.

I could see she started thinking about it, though, and, for asking honestly, she told me something back. "I wanted my grandmother to come that day. She was willing, but Cannon he say No. Didn't want her. Say y'all ought to see 'young strong black people clamoring at the gates.' My grandmother she say, Son I been clammering sixty-seven years on those gates. Then she went in the kitchen and shut the door on him."

Geneece threw me a sideways glance. "That was your mama playing the piano?"

When we got to the welcome mat, she stood on it hump-shouldered. Mr. Baxevanis opened the door smiling; he wore a scarf at his neck tucked into a starched white shirt I'd picked up at the dry cleaners. His smile froze. "Oh God!" he cried and pulled Geneece in. "Was that Pete's Thunderbird at the corner? He circled for an hour yesterday! Hurry, they'll see us!"

At that Geneece's eyes went stony and she turned around. I knew I should have done all this before, but I hadn't: I explained to her, in a quick whisper, as Mr. Baxevanis slammed and locked the door, that his sister and brother were after him, and why. "No lie?" Geneece's shoulders came down; she looked interested. An agitated Mr. Baxevanis ushered us to the couch, and hustled into the kitchen. On the top wires of her cage, Josephine Baker beat her wings.

Geneece craned her head, taking in the parrot, then the rest of the room. "Kinda dim in here," she squinted suspiciously. "Why it so dim in here?"

"We play like I'm on stage, and he sits back there in the theatre."

"What you talking about?"

"We pretend like it's the New York theatre. Mr. Baxevanis used to belong to a theatre club. He took up tickets every Saturday night for thirteen years."

"Oh." She settled the notebook on her lap. "He the one give you that poem, huh."

By the time he brought us lemonade on a tray, sighing, "Wrong again, my life story," Mr. Baxevanis was breathing naturally. Geneece sat with her feet together and her back not touching the couch. She and I might never have exhanged a word. Mr. Baxevanis didn't notice; he sat down right in front of her on the ottoman, and spoke to her confidentially. Geneece edged back her toes.

"All right. Geneece, Mayda needs a nudge. She says you're very good, so I thought you might be an influence on her."

"I cannot stay very long," Geneece said.

"Well then let's get started," Mr. Baxevanis resettled himself in the dark and crossed his legs. "I'm an expert audience."

Geneece flipped her notebook to a page, stood, then looked out at him. "I can't read my pencil writing."

"Oh, the lamp, the lamp!" He leapt up, tossed off the shade, switched on the bulb, and pointed at her.

As in class, Geneece located her distant spot over Mr. Baxevanis's head and inhaled.

"Oh no, no, look at me, please!"

Startled, she threw me a half-mean look, and Mr. Baxevanis a stubborn one.

"Directly into my eyes now."

Geneece began again, dutifully gazing toward Mr. Baxevanis, though the bright light must have bothered her. She said part of Reverend King's "I Have a Dream" speech. She stopped and she started with rests, with rushes, all those things Mr. Baxevanis wanted me to learn. She ended with that one verse of "America the Beautiful," and she sang it. She was great. When she finished she sat down, stiffer than ever.

Shadowy behind the naked light bulb, Mr. Baxevanis said only, "Again, please."

Geneece protested, "It's Mayda's turn."

He ignored that. "Surely you understand I'm just waiting to be moved? I want you to move me. Now, look at me this time. Don't be afraid, and don't half do it. Let yourself go."

Geneece's mouth twitched, but she rose and began again.

"Let go," Mr. Baxevanis interrupted.

After a few more lines, he broke in again, "Make me hear it, Geneece!" It was like heckling except that he seemed excited. He called "Geneece!" like a threat and a cheer for her at the same time.

Geneece's gripped hands broke apart. Her shoulders shifted and her ankles forgot to line up. Her voice came alive. She had to catch her breath when she sat down.

Mr. Baxevanis clapped and hurrahed. Geneece went back to holding herself stiff but she looked pleased. Mr. Baxevanis crowed, "I could be a teacher, couldn't I? Mayda, don't you think so? Lydia would die." His index finger ordered me.

"Now, you, Mayda. Where's your costume?"

I tied the scarf and faced the cone of light. For a second I was quiet, regretting that I would never be as good as Geneece. But then she dragged the ottoman out into the audience by Mr. Baxevanis. She put her elbows on her knees and leaned forward so intently; her low voice urging *C'mon now Mayda* came all around me so that I saw home was rare and not a place. I looked into my audience, and began. I had made it past the woman hiding treasures in her garden, and was almost to the strength of two hearts when someone rapped on the door. Geneece and Mr. Baxevanis had been paying such close attention, they flinched. Knocking became pounding.

"Andreas! . . . know . . . in there!" Knuckles rattled the window next to the door.

Mr. Baxevanis waved at me to check the shutters. I did; he'd gotten them all, except for the far window by the door. He hurried over to it. I peered out from the dark living room into the foyer, toward the window. They'd see me if I got too close. Two dark heads were bobbing out there; they must have been stepping all over the shrubbery.

Mr. Baxevanis had his hands clasped before his chest. "Please stop this. Have I bothered either of you? Have I ever tried to hurt you in any way?"

"You . . . fair, Andreas? . . . take the subpoena!"

"Pete, be reasonable. You own two restaurants. Lydia got Aunt Irene's duplex. Lydia's got a pension. Pete, what did I have?"

"Take . . . now," Pete growled with his mouth close to the window. "Or we . . . county sheriff!"

Miss Baxter's alto voice joined her brother's. "Mama never meant . . . not of sound mind at the end, Andreas!"

Geneece sprang up from the ottoman when she heard Miss Baxter. "What that bitch doing here," she said.

I sank down in Mr. Baxevanis's director's chair. "That's his sister."

Mr. Baxevanis was pleading, "Mama was clear as a bell! Look, I sent you the furniture, the ceramics, the fur coat, everything. She left me the house, Lydia, and I'm keeping it."

"His sister is her?" Geneece looked toward me.

Mr. Baxevanis heard, and pinned me with a wild look. "You didn't tell her?"

Miss Baxter's voice threatened. "Who's . . . Got a friend . . . Andreas? Sheriff might like . . . "

Geneece accused us, "Y'all put me in a bad place." She

picked up an ash tray, a clear heavy glass with points like a starfish. Then, as though reprimanded by some authority in her ear, slowly, reluctantly, she set it down again.

Mr. Baxevanis threw up a hand at the window and glared at me as he rushed over to Geneece. "If I did not need allies I would kill Mayda now. Please forgive this . . ." he waved both hands, "this horrible family drama. I swear on my mother's grave it has nothing to do with you." He raised two fingers in some kind of backwards Boy Scout pledge.

From the chair I whispered, "Mr. Baxevanis . . ."

He made an ax motion. To Geneece he said, "I am so very sorry for this unpleasantness." He wheeled on me. "She had the right to know before she chose to come here. Why didn't you let her know?" Geneece stared at me, too, hard-mouthed.

"But I wanted her to come . . ." Bill was right, I was stupid, but I said it anyway, what I meant. ". . . and play with us."

The little nets beneath Mr. Baxevanis's eyes weighed down.

"Look we're not doing anything," I tried, "so they can't do anything to us."

Geneece muttered, "Yeah, uh huh." We knew they already had. They'd wrecked our New York theatre. They'd spattered the books and the rugs and us with ugliness.

There was an awful blow, and a crack from the window, then in a thick shrieky voice, Pete yelled, ". . . think you're our brother. You're not our brother!"

Mr. Baxevanis's head snapped up; his spine arched. It was as if Pete had thrown something and hit him in the back. Josephine, hunkered on the roof of her cage like a householder in a flood, shrilled, *Break the will! Prettygirl!* "Oh untrue, untrue," Mr. Baxevanis murmured, his chin mashed in and quivering.

Geneece yanked my shoulder.

I jumped up, ripping the silly, flimsy scarf off my hair.

"All right I should have told you, I shouldn't ever have asked you here, I give up!"

Her mean eyes were not even looking at me. "Don't do nothing against them sorry people, Mayda. But . . ." her jaw began its dangerous slide, ". . . you might could get yourself that lamp. Just for in case." An explosion of glass shocked our ears; Pete's loud curses streamed in. He knew what he'd find, what filth was going on in his own mother's house . . .

Two red patches burned through Mr. Baxevanis's sagging cheeks; slowly, he doubled his fists.

I grabbed the lamp, prisms quaking, and ran back. Geneece's gaze was locked on the window as on thundering Romans. Imitating her stance, I fixed my feet solidly on the azure carpet. What small fists Mr. Baxevanis had. Practical, he'd called the woman scrabbling in her blue garden, passionate, not one to yield up dear things. I set down my weapon and caught his wrists. I moved his thumbs to the outside, so if it came to a fight, they would not be broken.

# Cold in the Bone

ONE EVENING AS my parents were gearing up to fight about Grandma, Captain Sam Maynard dropped by. After an odd hesitation when they saw their old friend's face at the door, no more than a startled beat, my parents sat him down, my father spouting baseball scores while my mother clattered the percolator together and lashed dust from the good cups with matching saucers. She brought out the lemon icebox pie we'd had for dessert. Then, excusing herself, she led Grandma to the bathroom. Afterward, she plugged her under the electric blanket so Grandma would not interrupt the visit by hollering for someone to cover her up because she was cold in the bone.

Grandma was actually my father's grandmother. Though until tonight neither of my parents had said anything definite, their faces wore a helplessness that told me she was with us for good. Which did not logically stand to be eons in any case—I was surprised it fell to me to point out the obvious: Grandma was ninety-seven years old. Ma jabbed her finger, countering. She recalled Grandma claiming her own grandfather had lived to 104. Ma looked desperate at the thought of seven more years of Grandma. You couldn't wholly condemn her. You had to balance her callousness

*25*

against her burden—my father and me and Kevin, my older, doing-bad-in-school brother to worry about, late-night phone stupidities from my alcoholic uncle, Ma's baby brother, and a permanent weariness accumulated last summer when her own mother lingered on the cancer ward, her skin changing with the leaves from pale olive to a dirty, final yellow. Ma was at a battered point in her life.

A visit from Sam Maynard usually rendered her bright and scattered but for some reason that was not happening tonight. I had gleaned that before the cataclysm of Pearl Harbor, they were to some degree sweet on one another. In his presence a what-if blush would seep up her neck. She asked questions simply in order to attach his name to them: Really, *Sam*, is that so? My father acted very welcoming to him, very friendly, as though to prove bygones were long bygone or what a broad man he was or that he had Ma while Sam Maynard, poor old bachelor soldier, lay down to sleep on a single bed you could bounce a quarter on.

Captain Maynard took his coffee black and talked about a dead soldier named Buddy Lewis, who, in his superiors' considered opinion, the army never should have taken.

"What was his problem?" Dad looked primed to hear about somebody else's problem.

Captain Maynard brought his hands up behind his head. He had big shoulders still, wider than my father's. "They thought all that boy's dogs didn't bark, if you know what I mean."

"So why did they keep him?" Ma asked, but without throwing in a Sam, just so she could slide her tongue over it.

By the time they discovered that, Captain Maynard said, they also saw how Buddy Lewis could shoot and glide through an obstacle course and generally endure and then they couldn't cut off their nose without spiting their face. "His folks were squirrel-eaters from up north of here. Kid spent all his life hunting the Big Thicket." As he was poised to bite into a forkful of pie, a move my mother usually blatantly waited for, a horror crept over Captain Maynard's face. "Godamighty, Warren," he exclaimed to my father, "you aren't kin to any of them up there, are you?" He thought he had set his boot square in his mouth because our name was Lewis, too.

You could see Dad get a free plug out of the captain's discomfort but he assured him we were no relation. We'd just read the notice in the paper, like everybody else.

"But don't you know the girl he was married to?" my mother asked me.

"Sarah Fitch married a boy named Lewis. I guess it was him. Poor Sarah."

"Kinda unfortunate girl." Captain Maynard grimaced and touched his face, as if to dent in the skin there like Sarah Fitch's skin was dented, but no imitation could do justice to the real thing. He shoveled icebox pie and winked an acknowledgment to my mother, who absorbed this puny tribute like an indrawn breath but with none of the usual flush around her jawline. Then he wiped his fingers on a paper napkin and told us about this soldier with the same name as us.

Buddy Lewis was a brown-haired boy with an overhung brow and eyes so deepset he looked blind or retarded, which was apparently what the officers of E Company took him for. He was a hunkerer, hunkered to eat or to wait, with a pure, blank-eyed patience, elbows propped on his knees, hands dangling. His accent got laughed at—before they took him out in the bush. E Co. discovered that Buddy Lewis was a swamp man. He could sleep in the rain. Tolerated the heat, the soggy ground, the bugs, grinned at leeches before setting a match under them, would twirl a snake barehanded. He had a grace moving through water, and he would wade anything. One day, out from a place called Swan Lock—or that's what it sounded like—Buddy hunkered down by the roots of a teak tree and wouldn't budge. The sergeant got out of him that VC "done been here" and kept on him about how he knew. Buddy wrinkled his nose, shrugged. A pall descended, everybody holding their own piece of ground, the point man stuck out there a ways and gazing back at them like from a far country. After a while Buddy waved him wide to the right. He needed no other direction, faded wide between the trees and floated back without setting foot to earth. Buddy started chunking cans, spiced beef and turkey loaf, parsing out his throws till the wire tripped.

It did not take two demonstrations to establish Buddy's value. Forward-thinkers, E Co. kept their mouths shut—all except the young lieutenant who couldn't help recounting in the officers' hooch the spiced beef rolling and bouncing and *boom*! He told it a couple of times before his men heard and throttled him quiet. Too damn late.

Buddy started getting borrowed. At first pieces of paper changed hands, one lieutenant to another, semi-official non-sense. Then outright bogus. Then two or three of a company's stump-necked men would just appear—they always sent the big ones—casting a wedged-shaped shadow on his bunk. Bravo or Delta or Tango—they were going out and they wanted Buddy.

Buddy would tie his boots, gather his gear, merge into their shadow. Word was instead of changing every two hours he could walk point or slack for most of a day without his nerve snapping but if he was slack don't give him the com-pass and for sure not a map. Buddy thought maps were funny. Didn't need them, maybe couldn't read them, and would mess with your head—making up dumb coordinates which turned out to be Greenland or Bombay or New Iberia, Loui-siana or the Bering Straits. But they came back, bringing Buddy hollow-cheeked and blistered, deepset eyes red from dope and reading what he could read which was the land in all its rooted and bare and watered and grassy form. They

came back from the teak forest or the abandoned rubber plan-
tations or the paddies or clearcuts overgrown again—with
tales of a mined trail or a VC ville avoided; of a sniper Buddy
located by smell; of Buddy yelling at a man who maybe a
second later tripped a Chicom grenade . . . and given the
wealth of five seconds to outrun it, the man did. They all
came back. Two months, three months, four, Swan Lock was
a safe place, a magic place, Buddy Lewis its living charm.

Until a helicopter and a genuine paper arrived. Causing
a spontaneous uprising—the chopper had to shake them off
the skids to take Buddy away. There would be more choppers later, the black horse of Air Cav wanted Buddy and so
did the 25th, E Co. heard of him out by The Pineapple in the
mounds and ditches, and they heard the enemy had heard
about him, too, up in the reddish-yellow dirt and the scrub
and the deadly villes of Cu Chi. Always more choppers and
more land curved or canopy-shaded or ascending in mist-
green levels or stretching flat or wet, and finally *the* chopper,
blasted out of the sky. Back at Swan Lock everybody agreed
they had to go after him in the air, didn't they, in that track-
less place, because they'd never have got Buddy on the
ground.

"All she wrote," Sam Maynard said.

Dad said, "I'll be damned."

Shaking her head, my mother wondered how the widow
was taking it. Sam Maynard shifted around and admitted
this was just what had filtered back from guys-who-knew to
other-guys-who'd-heard to him, not exactly the kind of information the widow would have been given. He mentioned
the favor he'd done, which was to get her admitted back
into her right grade at the high school so she could finish
along with her class and support the child in a halfway decent manner.

I was still seeing pineapples and horrible thin wires but it
did get through he'd said Sarah Fitch would be returning to

school. In my grade. I wanted to know how in the world she could come back as a junior when she'd dropped out in the tenth grade.

Sam Maynard tugged at the crease in his trousers. He said Superintendant Williams had cut some slack. This was not common knowledge, but Mr. Williams had a boy missing that hadn't been found yet. He was sure they would though, they'd find him and he would be just fine. Captain Maynard's loud honest voice slicked into a practiced tone.

That slickness made me remember what my parents had remembered as soon as they laid eyes on him: Sam Maynard was the newsman.

He was the one who'd rung the bell at Perry Parsons' when Perry lost his legs. They said he was set to knock on doors in the colored neighborhoods, too—with the army car and his dress uniform, the telegram and a pair of strong arms to catch anybody who went down. Dad flicked a sharp glance at Ma. This is what it said: The superintendant was probably so relieved Sam Maynard wasn't there in his official capacity that if pressed, he'd have rustled up a blank form and typed out the widow's diploma himself.

Later, my parents got into a fight anyway over why Dad didn't offer Sam Maynard a glass of Wild Turkey. Really they were still jangled about Grandma and—neither one wanting to open that wriggling can again—they had to finish some way. Dad flung open the door to the hall, pointing toward the end room where my brother—failer of English and Biological Science—studied weird books that had nothing to do with school or leafed through a beatnik newspaper (Dad's adjective) delivered by mail. Huh? Dad said, huh? He'd already won; Ma's mouth slammed shut but he said it anyway. Dad said Sure, they'd known Sam Maynard twenty years, Ma even longer and no doubt more biblically, but no etiquette he knew required him to drink whiskey with Port Sabine's designated angel of death.

His yelling woke Grandma. Ma smiled evilly and headed in the other direction. "Goddamnit," Dad muttered, and looked at me, so I went on in to her.

GRANDMA WAS IN the bed snuffling, brushing away tears with her fists. Her little rack of shoulders shook. They were so thin, her shoulders, depleted of all but skin draped loose on chalky bone; behind them where I could not see her spine curved cruelly. She wanted water so I used the toothpaste cup from the sink. She wouldn't notice the white smears down its side because she couldn't see that well and she liked water that tasted vaguely sweet and minty.

I held the cup but Grandma got it on her anyway. She was an inefficient swallower. "Is that enough?" I asked her.

She said Yeah, swiping her fist across her top lip. Because she lay in bed a lot, the back of her hair was whorled away from her skull.

"Is Papa gone?" she said.

You had to understand this about her: She took any scariness for "Papa." In this case she meant Dad, who'd upset her yelling about Sam Maynard.

"Papa's gone, Grandma."

"Good."

She didn't seem to need anything else but now she was awake. "You wanna talk, Grandma?"

"Yeah," she said.

"Well what do you say?"

"Is Papa dead?"

"Six foot under. I promise."

She nodded but still looked out at me alertly like a squirrel from a cage. She kept her mouth wide open, curled almost in a smile. Ma's comment on this mannerism was that Grandma's breath would float the Russian navy. But really she looked poised on the point of saying some glad thing.

You just had to be reconciled that she'd never say it. I found it ironic that Ma with all her burdens didn't appreciate the brilliant resource we had in Grandma. She was the perfect person to talk to. She would listen to anything and she would never judge or warn you.

"You want me to talk?" I asked her.

"Yeah."

"Okay." So I told her about my new and pinching concern, which none of the adults had even thought of: that Sarah Fitch, poor Buddy Lewis's widow, would now return to school as Sarah Lewis.

Sarah Lewis was my name, and I had it first. I felt encroached upon. I felt taken away from. I foresaw confusion, comparisons, and worse, ridicule.

I described to Grandma how from the back, Sarah had a regular girl's body and hair that fell to her waist, sunny brown in color. But when she turned around, it was a shock. Sarah had the kind of acne known as "disfiguring." It had stained the skin of her face and neck gradations of purple and red, dug channels, left satiny tumorous mounds and eroded pits. It came on her about the seventh grade, and the next year we studied the Middle Ages. When we got to the part about the Black Plague, the running sores and the terrible "buboes," the deadly pus bursting onto the hands of the healthy, everyone in the class looked at Sarah except the teacher who was deliberately not looking. Sarah had on a sleeveless dress that day and you could see the acne had sprouted onto her shoulders now in solid red lumps. You could feel the whole class gauging where it stopped, if it did.

"I found out, Grandma. By accident."

I was up on the bank of the Lower Sabine canal late in the afternoon of a July day, pretending to be blind. I had closed my eyes and limited myself to feeling. My balance went, the ground veered and shifted, leery of me. I could hear laughter somewhere far off, and a breeze fit tight around my neck and underneath my hair. I said, This is how it is, this nothing, this airy black box.

Quick I opened my eyes and pulled the world over me again. The sky was washed blue. The treeline across the canal cast a hundred shades of green, with here and there a dark opening like a hole you could enter standing up. An egret on the far bank plodded into the air for a few feet and plunked itself down. A crow passed over and as if to emphasize the comfort of sight, the egret turned its loopy neck and watched the crow fly. The old canal was just a wide trough of brown water. Limber brown wavelets streamed by. The sun lit them and the wind blew them along. After a while my blood pulled with the waves. Again I heard laughing and, holding out my arms, I skimmed the big pipe over to the swampy side of the canal. I crossed a mowed strip and tiptoed down into the weedy grass to the blackish opening in the trees.

From where I stood I thought it was two colored kids horsing around in the standing water. I froze there at the edge of the tall damp grass, as though, instead of me spying on them, they had trapped me. They were naked. I'd never seen a colored girl's hair so long, matted and mudded in ropy strips. The girl was hoisted onto the boy's shoulders, her hands in his hair. She grabbed onto a vine as the boy waded away, legs plowing from the water. He tried to break her grip. Straining, she held on, her brown body arched backward. He walked out from beneath her and let her fall.

When she stood up, laughing, I saw the girl's face, her body streaked white. They weren't colored. They were caked in mud. I didn't recognize the boy. But the girl was Sarah Fitch, ribby and long-muscled, her nipples peaked like flowercaps that close at night. Except for the dark between her legs, her body was as white and unmarked as any girl's. Squatting, she thrust her hands down in the water, patted more mud on her face, and leapt onto the boy's back wrapping her arms and legs around him. He carried her through the water, sure of his footing. From the side, a thickness poked out from the boy's thighs that she moved to rub with her foot and that stopped him, his head falling back in a slow posture of thanksgiving. When he shifted her around to his front I turned and ran. I didn't care if they heard. I was scared and I wanted away from them. I had a deep and exact knowledge of what they were about to do and I did not know how I knew that, and that scared me, too.

That was the summer after ninth grade and Sarah Fitch did not come but a month to the tenth.

"I really ran, Grandma."

She said, "Yeah."

She made no move to lie down. So I told her a fairy tale. It had a mermaid with sore feet and some sandcrabs and mullet as her kindly helpers, and a prince and a wicked, wicked king. She liked the repetition in it and the drama and the voices, and she liked hearing about animals. She lay right back to sleep then but I made her roll to the other side. She always curled to sleep on the left with her heart down against the mattress. That preference had caused an open sore to wear on her left hip, which Ma doctored with ointment. Left alone, it would eat clear through her.


WIDOWED SARAH LEWIS came back to school on a blowy September day. Sixty miles away, a hurricane was churning up the Gulf. I watched her stand on the sidewalk waiting for the bell, the only still person among dozens of kids grouped in twos and threes and more, stomping and shoving around. They were blurs and she was clear. Sarah hugged a blue cloth notebook and bowed her head to hide her face, but the wind kept whipping her hair back and showing it anyway.

Since our seats were assigned alphabetically, she sat in front of me in Miss Weisbach's English class. "We got the same name now," Sarah said to me that first day. She peeked out from her hair to see if I minded.

"Yeah, I know," I said. I did mind; I scrawled my name across the top of a fresh page, making large possessive loops of the S and the L. Rain pelted the windows.

It was a couple of weeks before she said anything else aloud and then that was unintentional. Miss Weisbach had been pulling her flat blonde hair out, trying to get us to talk. We'd read "The Big Two-Hearted River" and were mired in silence as in deep mud. Kenny Farmer's textbook splattered to the floor and he reeled sideways to pick it up then scrabbled to find the page we were on. Dead quiet again.

"You've read this story? You've all read it?" Miss Weisbach demanded.

Kenny stared far into his book.

Linda Meyers finally raised her hand and said she thought this story was a big waste of paper. A few other girls agreed with her. Unpredictable Miss Weisbach didn't get mad—she looked cheered to hear some talking.

Jim Tate—he never asked permission, he just spoke up— said the fishing part was nice, though. It sounded to him like the guy knew what he was writing about.

Cecile Jenkins raised her hand. She was a beanpole colored girl whose manner reminded me of a middle-aged woman's, someone bogged and troubled like my own mother, because she was so solemn. Miss Weisbach called on her but Cecile waited until the teacher nodded for her to talk. "I think this story's about the war," she said. She stopped again and Miss Weisbach had to nod again to get her going.

"This man he's been in the war and he's glad to be out of it. That's why he has such a good time fishing. Because he's out of the war."

Miss Weisbach looked like Cecile had handed her a bouquet of sweetheart roses.

"See here at the end it says . . ." Cecile read the sentences at the end.

"I don't get it," Linda Meyers said. In front of me, Sarah turned in her seat so she could look out from her hair at the people who were talking, Cecile in particular.

Cecile frowned in concentration. "Well, it's like if something bad happens to you, then whatever else happens to you you remember the bad thing, too. Like . . . like . . . " Cecile drew a pencil from behind her ear, turning it end to end until she could think of something. My guess was she already had a personal example but she did not want to use it. Cecile said, "Like what if you were President Kennedy's kids and your daddy got killed like that. Every day of their lives Caroline and little John-John gonna know their daddy got killed like that even when they're playin or eatin."

The discussion haywired here. Any other teacher would have dragged us back to the subject at hand, but not Miss Weisbach.

"He was a good President," Janie Finlay piped up. "We're not like those kids in Dallas that were glad he was dead. We cried." She wanted Miss Weisbach to differentiate us from the murder-celebrating kids of Dallas, since Miss Weisbach was not from Port Sabine, or even from Texas. Miss Weisbach was from Minnesota.

"You cried," Jim Tate said, but he wasn't mean about it. He turned in his seat like Sarah had, angled out, fingering his pencil.

Everybody started to talk about it then, in an orderly way as though we were in line. It was different than school usually was because every single speaker received the dignity of being listened to. One by one the white kids talked. The colored kids except for Cecile stayed quiet. They went to this school but you could tell they didn't think of it as theirs yet. But finally Molly Giles, who I liked because outside of class I heard her laugh so much, told about her teacher Mrs. Washington weeping with a handkerchief draped over her face. Really, everybody's stories were about identical, the PA sputtering, the teachers' stricken announcements, us absorbing the shock of the grown people around us. The white kids were in Longfellow Elementary across the street, the colored kids across town in their school. We were still separate then.

Sarah followed each speaker intently. She held her head in that characteristic posture of hers, thrust out on her neck like she would not miss anything, not a word or a gesture, but ducked, lowered, and her eyes peered up and out at us.

Miss Weisbach told us about the time she saw President Kennedy ride down a boulevard.

"You saw him in real life?" Janie's eyes widened. We all wanted to hear about that but Miss Weisbach only described what we already knew, how young he looked, how bronze his hair in the sunshine, how tanned and smiling, how pleased he seemed to wave at the people thronging toward him.

Jim Tate asked what the President was riding in.

"A convertible."

Silently we took this in.

Donnie Ferris, a slouching colored boy who barely peeped at roll call, blurted, "They gone stop that. They gone cover up the cars from now on." His eyes flickered in dismay, whether over the vulnerability of convertibles or that he'd actually spoken to the whole class, you couldn't tell.

Out of the blue, Miss Weisbach asked, "Are we in history?"

Linda Meyers jumped on that one. "No, we're in English," she said and most people snickered. But not me because I didn't think Linda was all that funny and not Sarah because she didn't even seem to hear Linda's smart remark.

Cecile Jenkins' arm lifted. This time heads turned toward her. Miss Weisbach nodded and said, "Cecile?"

"Yes, ma'am." Cecile slipped her yellow pencil behind her ear. "We are."

"We are?" The bell underscored this soft, boggled exclamation from Sarah. People stood up, stacking books and note-books, laughing at her.

I slid out of my seat, too. But I noticed that as Cecile passed her, Sarah reached out to pull her sleeve. It was rude and needy, almost the gesture of an animal, a heavy paw swipe on Cecile. Sarah had her book open pointing at a line on the page. Cecile said something in that earnest way she had. As she nodded, she reminded me of someone. I was down the hall, through the breezeway, and appoaching the gym door before I could put my finger on who. It was Miss Weisbach, the perennial nodder and encourager. The teacher.

MY BROTHER KEVIN was allergic to teachers but he liked Port Sabine's old library downtown. That was the only place he was allowed to go when he was grounded, which, once the grades rolled in, was pretty much most of the time. Of all the buildings in our Pig Stand, 7-11, refinery town, the library was unique: built of dungeon-colored, jagged-cut rock, fit into turrets like the palace of a minor princess or a sand castle dripped from stone. Its strange, dim atmosphere spooked me, put me in mind of ancient laws, bogs, the brutal clanging of metal on metal. But it did not daunt Kevin.

One night Ma, delivering stacks of clean, folded clothes to our rooms, couldn't resist hovering over his shoulder. Poor Ma acted pitifully cheerful around him, like an old girlfriend who wants to show she's not hurt by his not liking her any-more. She asked what the numbers were all over his paper, geometry or what? Kevin explained he'd calculated her birth chart and she better watch out because Saturn was moving into her third house and she just might have trouble with siblings or short trips or even her mental . . . arrangements.

"Siblings?" Ma sounded gratified. Every Christmas she crammed a paperback dictionary in my brother's stocking; Kevin kept the latest on the back of the commode. "Wait, what do you mean my mental arrangements?"

"Oh, you know, just your perceptions, how you take in information about what happens to you," Kevin said.

"Perceptions?" Ma was getting worked up. "And you're doing geometry all on your own?"

"No, Ma, you do this stuff with trig." Kevin had always cruised through math but until he discovered these books he'd believed the most satisfying use for it was counting change. That's what he'd told me the week before when he figured my birth chart and pointed to my vacant first house, the house of Self.

"Trigonometry? Oh Kevin," Ma gushed, "why can't you do this with school? Just look what you could do if you tried!"

"I am trying." He herded her out and cranked Jefferson Airplane up, so she'd stay away.

Ma retreated to her sewing room. She hadn't sewed in years but she used to sit in there by herself anyway. But now the sewing room was Grandma's. Ma had forgotten that, like her mental arrangements were upset.

"Is it bad to have a vacant First House?" I'd wanted to disregard this piece of information; instead, I'd been brooding over it. I infiltrated Kevin's room, later, where he bent under the glow of his desk lamp. Pages of math scribblings lay around his record player. Kevin was using a protracter and repeatedly sticking the needle into the soft groove of "Comin' Back to Me." I inched up behind him as a perfect circle appeared on the paper. "Ah, your First House," he said, like he was some kind of wizard. He didn't look up. "Who are you?" he said.

"Your sister. Sarah. You dumbhead," I said over his shoulder. But I wasn't feeling derogatory, I was feeling sort of impressed.

"Who's Sarah?" he asked. He completed the circle, picked up a ruler, and laid it across the paper, edging it into place with his fingertips.

"What do you mean?"

"No," he said, "what do *you* mean?"

"C'mon, Kevin."

Kevin went off for fifteen minutes on the fateful transits of planets—how they orbited around influencing other planets and wreaking bad or good luck on you—and then on something called "karma." I could only manage to picture this as an intricate ledger with some deeds written in glinting golden strokes like a sparkler's, and others in blood. He would give me a fullscale reading, he said, when he knew enough; he tapped a stack of books beside his elbow on the desk. That might take months. Meanwhile, Kevin said, I should—like the rest of the menagerie—stay the hell out of his domain. He locked the door in my face, click.

Mr. Wizard wasn't the only person who could view the future. He'd been outside one night before school started, jimmying his screen with a screwdriver. I predicted that if I stayed awake to listen I would hear his window go up, sometime in the secret part of the night.


SARAH LEWIS INFILTRATED Miss Weisbach's domain, hanging around while the teacher tried to eat her lunch. I was Miss Weisbach's student aide and sometimes, as she ate a cheese sandwich and I recorded grades in her red book or copied out transparencies for the overhead projector, we used to talk, too. Me at a back desk and her at the big front one. It was nice, talking across the distance, and not at all like talking to Ma or Dad. You felt older, not younger, when you talked with Miss Weisbach. She didn't have time for me, though, once Sarah started showing up.

Sarah must have given up on her own lunch period; she was too shy to nudge her tray next to anybody. I'd heard nobody sat with her, either, except, a few times, Edward Fortner, the weirdest boy in school—famous for covering his portion of the lunch table with a red and white tablecloth. They knew each other from Chorus, where Edward's round head, thin shaggy hair, and minimal features made him look like a singing coconut.

The first time Sarah lurked in Miss Weisbach's door, I heard Miss Weisbach say, "Well, hi there," and Sarah blurt, "I never used to think about it but now I do. And I know when I could a been in history."

Miss Weisbach nodded. "And?"

"And it was when my husband Buddy went to the war. Because wars are history. So even if I was still here . . ." Sarah craned around meaning here in Port Sabine where we all believed there was no history, ". . . it had reached me."

Miss Weisbach could look Sarah in the face, maybe that was why Sarah liked her. She said, "It reached you a lot."

Sarah agreed. A dark flicker crossed her face, I thought. I wasn't sure. But it was enough to make me wonder how Sam Maynard had broken the news when he knocked on her door. How much did she know of that story he told us? Did she scream or just accept it? Or did she ask Sam Maynard question after question just to keep him talking until she could understand Buddy was dead? Maybe she ducked her head like she did in school—except not from shyness but for a shelter, so this stranger she didn't invite to her door couldn't watch the tears dripping off her cheeks. All I know is that after the flicker passed, she didn't show any more signs of grief that I could see. Just a relief to lean up against Miss Weisbach's doorframe, an eagerness, like she could have stood there talking through every class.

It was embarrassing what Sarah would reveal to Miss Weisbach. Her voice was quiet but I could still hear her, there in the back, and so could anyone else—like smartass Linda Meyers—doing make-up work. Once Sarah told Miss Weisbach she used to believe some of the kids in school were not real in the same way she was.

41

"What do you mean, not real?" Miss Weisbach asked.

It turned out Sarah meant that some kids were like the lifesize cardboard placards of movie stars in a theatre lobby. It was okay to look but you couldn't actually talk to them. Hearing that made me feel lonely, but Linda Meyers put one finger up to her head and circled it in the air. I think Miss Weisbach caught that. Not Sarah, she gave all her attention straight to Miss Weisbach's eyes.

Another day Sarah said, "When I was little, my mother used to go on trips. I learned to cook and fix my hair and all by myself."

Miss Weisbach didn't inquire about the trips, like anybody else would have, and which I mulled over. Instead, she asked Sarah didn't she mind being alone at night.

Sarah said not so much if she went around the house and touched everything. Or sang with the radio. She knew the verses to a million songs and how all the tunes should go. She used to fall asleep singing with the radio.

Miss Weisbach called her a problem-solver. Sarah didn't get what this meant. I didn't understand either.

"I mean, you analyze situations," Miss Weisbach explained. "Then you find an answer to your problem."

Oh, Sarah said, if you ponder on it, there is always one thing you can do. Always one thing. And then you do it and you feel better. Like you can untangle your hair by brushing the bottom part first. She stared at Miss Weisbach's blonde hair which was not bouffant like the other teachers' but straight and hanging. She looked like she wanted to brush it for her.

One day after school, when her mother—or some woman with long gray hair in a skinned-back pony tail—drove up in an old Ford, Sarah scooped a bundle from the front seat. She started out for the steps where Miss Weisbach was stationed on after-school duty. But just then the assistant principal called the teacher's name and crooked his finger at her so she went back inside. That left Sarah with one foot poised on the bottom step, like she didn't know whether to wait for Miss Weisbach or to trail back to the car with her baby unadmired. She just stood there with her bundle with no one to look at it, stranded.

The people standing closest to her were a bunch of blond-haired sophomore boys who thought they were surfers. You knew they were not about to go coochi-coo a baby. The next closest were the colored kids waiting for the nine bus. I felt sorry for Sarah but irritated with her, too. It was like she was made of glass. You always had to see what she was feeling— and it made you squirm. I looked away from her.

When I glanced up again, Cecile Jenkins was walking toward her, with her brother Delton in tow. Cecile stopped on one corner of Sarah. Delton tugged free of his sister's grasp and took Sarah's other side. Molly Giles trailed up, right in front. For a few minutes Sarah was anchored on three sides, surrounded. She just lit up. I couldn't hear what they said but Cecile messed with the blanket and Molly leaned in babbling in a high voice; she must have been pretending to be the baby talking. Delton offered some remark, and Sarah beamed, smiling down on her own baby like she was the one who hadn't seen it before. Her knees dipped. If her mother hadn't laid hard on the horn then, she would have poured all over the sidewalk.

Some time after that I was filling in test grades, shading my work with a paper so Linda Meyers couldn't spy on it. Linda was diddling over a punishment essay titled "What's Good About Listening." Her first sentence read: "I like it when people listen to me." With a quieter voice than usual, Sarah told Miss Weisbach she'd had a colored friend once, when they were both little girls, but when her mother found out she said Sarah couldn't play with her anymore. Sarah said, "She's my own mama but I have to say she's mean about all that. All people are some part mean, aren't they, Miss

Weisbach?"

Miss Weisbach agreed that people could be mean.

Sarah said, "Maybe not Cecile. Or Delton."

"So they're not like those kids you couldn't talk to? The kids you thought looked like cardboard pictures of movie stars?" Miss Weisbach smiled at her, to let her know that idea was silly.

Sarah's head lifted. "They're colored."

Behind her hand, Linda Meyers said, *Duh*. Did Miss Weisbach think you would find glamourous cutouts of Cecile Jenkins decorating a movie lobby? Where had she been?

Minnesota, I whispered.

Miss Weisbach told Sarah that she'd already figured out for herself Cecile was a nice person. Hadn't she? Already figured it out for herself?

"Yes, ma'am, I did that." Sarah ducked her head again. "Sometimes," she said, "I feel like the world was ruined before we got ahold of it."

This remark only made Miss Weisbach look serious. She said, "So what do you do about that, Sarah?"

"Me?" Sarah flattened a hand against her breastbone to indicate herself. "Oh I ain't the kind that fixes anything."

Miss Weisbach just shrugged like she wasn't so sure. Which made Sarah smile and turn away, looking out into the hall. Like the very idea that she might affect the world in any way at all had literally turned her head.

Linda Meyers took to repeating these conversations. She was secretary of The Thespians Club. She developed an act: Miss Weisbach, nibbling laterally across a sandwich like an ear of corn while Sarah leaned against the doorframe, straining her brow. Linda exaggerated every detail. She made Sarah look like an idiot, like a cave woman. Like someone who'd never had a conversation before and was beside herself to find words meant the same thing to someone else as they meant to her. Linda propped her temple against her index finger and let her jaw hang, a parody of Sarah's having a thought. "Ain't the world ruined?" Linda'd say. She had a successful career until she embellished one performance by dragging her fingertips down her cheeks as though blemishing her own white skin—and a boy she liked winced and turned away. She got her laughs, but they were guilty laughs, some of them.

Sarah would occasionally wander over to Cecile Jenkins where she waited for the nine bus, folded over her books, a jumble of forearm and long gleaming shinbone. Some of the white kids joked about Sarah and her new friend, while the other colored kids waiting there just drifted sideways into their own jostling circles. Cecile would answer some question of Sarah's, gesturing more naturally out there than she did in the classroom. She'd finish talking and stash her pencil behind her ear. Sarah, kneeling or squatting next to her— she never outright sat down—seemed to inhale everything Cecile said. She started showing up for English class with a pencil stuck behind her ear, poking through her long straight hair.

MA WAS DOWN in the mouth about her 44th birthday in October. "Now the days turn dark and short," she said. We all looked at her. Though my uncle had been calling late on Saturday nights to cry on Ma's shoulder about his stingy girlfriend or his numbskull boss, he forgot about her birthday. He didn't even send a card.

Grandma didn't know to give Ma anything but you couldn't blame her for that; she sat on the couch with her good expectant smile. I gave Ma a Whitman's Sampler. Grandma and I ate a few chocolates; I was careful to pick out the creams. Vanilla and raspberry, yum. But Kevin had thought ahead. Figuring he'd be grounded, he had ordered stuff from his newspaper and the J.C. Penney catalog. He gave Ma a small box wrapped in Christmas paper and decorated with a sticker instead of a bow. The round white sticker was outlined in black, pierced through the middle by a black, upside-down Y with an extra line drawn from the fork of it. I didn't think it was very festive. I thought he could have colored it or something. Ma looked uncertain when he told her it was a peace sticker but she melted when she saw the necklace nested in cotton—rhinestones in the shape of a tiny heart.

Excited, Dad stepped up with his present, or rather, shooed Ma into the kitchen where he had been all morning, setting it up. She walked in and stared at the flowing reeds, the diver, the bubbles, the graceful angel fish. Her neck bowed. She picked up the cylinder of fish food and read the little print on the outside of it. In a measured voice she said she could see she'd have to feed the fish—but just explain to her how often the aquarium would have to be cleaned. Dad ran down the whole deal about the gravel and algae and moving the fish while fresh water was added, being careful to rinse all soap from the sides of the glass. You only had to do it every month or so. He hoped she'd enjoy watching it while she cooked.

When Ma turned around she was crying. She said she couldn't believe Dad had given her another thing to take care of.

Dad was crushed, then pissed.

While the fight went on in their bedroom, Kevin and I sifted out flakes and watched the angelfish swarm up to them, gulping. We let Grandma help. We praised her when she got most of them in the water. Hey, good, we said, loudly. We overdid it, covering up the ugly voices, so she wouldn't get scared and ask about Papa. Grandma's vacant pleasantness became a true smile. We didn't realize what we were starting. From then on, she would totter in daily and then, on her unsteady way back, announce to whoever was sitting in the living room that she had fed the fish. It sort of became her job.

You would have thought Ma would like that, one less job she had to do, but it annoyed her. It was bizarre—she acted jealous. Maybe she felt that Grandma did one dinky task and got congratulated, while the only time Ma got noticed was when she didn't iron a pile of Dad's shirts or buy the car new tires. But the aquarium really grew on Ma. It got to be a favorite thing of hers. I'd come in after school and not find her talking back to "Jeopardy." She'd be sitting on the kitchen counter with a package of ground meat in her hands, watching the angelfish travel the silent water.

BY BAD LUCK the school Open House was on a night Dad had invited some people to dinner. Ma had got herself all dressed up. She had put a roast with potatoes and carrots in the oven but she was worried about hors d'oeurves, the cheese puff items that have to be baked at the last minute. She told Dad to go to the Open House with me and Kevin. Dad said he'd rather tackle the cheese puffs than the teachers. Kevin said he had to stay home in the back yard; he might even sleep out there. Tonight Mars was conjunct the moon in the constellation of Sagittarius. He wanted to observe that, and besides—

"Astronomy, huh?" Dad interrupted. "Maybe that's your science. Sure as hell wasn't biology."

"Besides," Kevin's voice sharpened, he was a senior and didn't need to go to any more Open Houses.

"You better pray that's true," Dad said.

Ma and I were ready to go when Grandma came out in her dress—her real dress, a navy blue one with covered buttons—and her navy blue purse that snapped at the top hanging open. She acted like she was going, too.

"Oh no," Ma said. "We have to walk to different classrooms, Grandma. It's too far for you."

Grandma looked at her and then at me. Usually her hair clumped like cotton balls glued sparsely on her head but now it fanned out in a nimbus. She had combed the top and sides of it. She fumblingly snapped her purse, looked up again, and took a step toward us.

"No," Ma said.

"Jesus, Loretta," Dad said.

Ma went into an unsolicited recitation—really a low caliber fit—about working the volunteer desk at the hospital all afternoon long, then rushing home to sling together the dinner and the cheese puffs and find and iron a table cloth, one that didn't have Christmas bells appliqued on it and—

"She could sit in Miss Weisbach's room," I said. "Miss Weisbach's really nice. We'll come back and get her."

So we took her. It was nuts but we did. Miss Weisbach had Koolaid and cookies, sat Grandma right behind her desk and made a big fuss over her. Grandma was happy. Ma and I trotted around to the various rooms receiving pleasant enough news about my grades. Then I deserted to sit with Grandma while Ma took a breath and set off to make the round of Kevin's classes. I didn't want to accompany that mission. I piled up three pecan sandies and brought some for Grandma.

I listened to Miss Weisbach talk to somebody's mother and use words like *thoughtful* and *persevering*, which described no one I knew, and then to the Skinners. Two parents waited to see her, a big colored man who'd wedged himself halfway into a school desk, and Jim Tate's mother who'd just walked in. When Miss Weisbach finished with the Skinners, these two both stepped up to her. "I believe I was next," the man said. Miss Weisbach smiled, "Yes, you were." Mrs. Tate seemed to grow taller; she strode over to study a poem thumb-tacked on the wall.

"Cecile Jenkins doing all right in your class?" the man

said. That pegged him. I decided Cecile didn't look at all like her father on the outside, she was wiry and light-boned, the kind of girl who twines one leg around the other like a vine. It was inside she carried that heaviness of his.

Miss Weisbach kept smiling even when he didn't return the smile. She launched into teacher language. Cecile was a pleasure to have in class. She had such an instinctive grasp of literature, etc., etc.

"We used to read books to her, now she reads all the time," Mr. Jenkins said, his voice softer.

Miss Weisbach rushed right into telling him how well Cecile interpreted a story—she meant "The Big Two Hearted River"—for the class, who didn't understand that the fishing trip in the story, that everything in the young man's present was shadowed by his painful war experience.

"Cecile, she would understand that. I was in the war. But that's nothing to talk about," Mr. Jenkins said. He didn't seem much affected by the nice things Miss Weisbach said about Cecile or by Miss Weisbach's enthusiasm, which had impressed my mother. He seemed almost offended in some way. "My daughter's just as smart as any child here," he added, like Miss Weisbach had said she wasn't. "She knows that now."

"She's very smart," Miss Weisbach nodded vigorously, a bit of bewilderment showing through her agreement. A light popped on in my head. What Mr. Jenkins didn't say was: she's just as smart as any white child. I could hear those unsaid words, even if Miss Weisbach couldn't.

In response maybe to Miss Weisbach's uncertain expression, Mr. Jenkins said, "But I just wanted to know was she doing all right."

"Oh yes," Miss Weisbach said, "she's earned one of the highest averages in the class." She said this almost like a question, as though she wasn't sure if such a good report would please Mr. Jenkins. But he seemed satisfied. Gravely he nodded. "I thank you then," he said. As he left, Mr. Jenkins also nodded to Mrs. Tate, who angled her rosy, pearl-decked neck away.

While Miss Weisbach was talking to Mrs. Tate, Ma dragged back in like she had arrows stuck all through her. "Underachiever," she mumbled, "underachiever, underachiever, underachiever. Let's go."

More parents, a couple and a mother by herself, entered and slid into the desks, the man joking about how badly he fit, patting his plaid shirt which gapped over the belly section.

I guess I helped Grandma up too fast. She was in the process of eating a sandy and she choked. She choked and coughed and then started sucking breath. Miss Weisbach whirled around. Ma and I hovered on either side of Grandma. The couple hurried over; Mrs. Tate just stared. "Is it a heart attack?" the man said. "Poor old biddy."

"No she's just choked." Ma flushed a little.

"Oh well then." He reached out to whack Grandma between the shoulder blades.

Ma yelled, "Don't, you'll break her back!" The man looked abashed and went and sat down. His wife lingered and helped us, once Grandma had begun to breathe all right again, sit her down at the desk. Miss Weisbach wanted to call an ambulance. Grandma had her hand cupped over her mouth. She took it off and looking at me, bared her gums in that way you see chimpanzees do. It wasn't that the man laughed, that would have been okay, we might all have laughed. What humiliated Ma was that he tried not to laugh. That he bent over and made noises against the desk.

"Look," I said, pointing to her teeth. Grandma had this upper outcropping of four or five teeth in front, spotted and carved into roundness like pebbles exposed to the elements. "Look, there's one missing. See?" Obligingly Grandma kept her mouth open; she liked the attention, I could tell. Ma and Miss Weisbach and the wife crowded around, peering in.

"Could she have swallowed it?" Ma asked me, like I would know.

"Swallowed a tooth?" the man said. Well, then, he guessed everything would come out all right . . . *in the end*. His shoulders were shaking. Ma's face flamed. His wife glared toward him and said, "Carl Meyers." So he was Linda Meyers' father. That made sense.

When we finally got home, the dinner guests were drinking highballs. Ma scraped up an expression for them. Her hair was not tidy. Dad had baked the cheese puffs okay and was crowing about that. He said Ma never gave him an ounce of credit.

I had to get Grandma ready for bed. I found, what with all the coughing, she'd wet her navy blue dress. Gross. She'd only done that once or twice before—it was the sheets she'd wet then—and I didn't think Ma needed to find out about this additional time. "Let's keep this between me and you," I said. "Okay Grandma? What do you say?" Grandma didn't care; she was so tired I had to lift her arms for her, and she called me Alice Ann. I didn't know anybody in our family named that.

I asked Dad when I went back out and sat down at the table. They had eaten only half the roast but I saw bitterly the potatoes were gone. Dad said Grandma had had an older sister named Alice Ann, who'd got consumption and died when she was twenty. He used his fingers, trying to calculate—she'd died at least . . .

"Like 80 years ago," Kevin said.

"Thereabouts," Dad said coolly. He didn't acknowledge Kevin's lightning calculation but rolled out a little of his grandmother's life for us and the guests. How her father lit out when Alice Ann passed on, leaving her to nurse a dying mother and care for the little ones. How, once the mother had passed, too, her father returned long enough to burn down the house for the insurance money. When she married and Grandpa signed on building roads through the piney woods, Grandma cooked for a twenty-man road crew and lived in a canvas tent. Gave birth to twins in one of those tents. "Once upon a time she was a force, that woman in there," Dad said, hooking his chin toward Grandma's room.

"She's a handful now," Ma said and smiled at the guests.

My brother got up and shoved his chair to the table. "Be a lot easier if she'd die," he said, "and you could just tell stories about her." That brought Dad right down on Kevin's head, the minute those people left.

THE MIXUPS, when they came, were not exactly Sarah Lewis's direct fault. It was just that you collided with her orbit and crappy things happened to you. Look at me and Kevin. Look at Delton Jenkins.

An assistant gym teacher called to say I didn't want to dress out for gym and was generally . . . well, not a joiner—was there a problem at home she should know about? Ma was cooking supper. She knew I liked playing games in gym but her disaster-antenna sprang up anyway. When you are at a battered point in your life, it is easy to believe bad things, even when you know better.

"What's this about you refusing to dress out for gym? Is this some kind of rebellion?" Ma blocked the door to my room, a spatula in hand. As a result of volunteering at the hospital after her mother's long stay there, she didn't wear aprons anymore. She said they made her feel tied up. Her pink and white volunteer smock was dusted with flour from the salmon croquettes, and her eyes were aggrieved.

"*You* I thought I could count on," she said. "I didn't think I had to worry about you. Mother said the same thing. The day she died. She said it was Kevin I'd—" Ma's voice dwindled as her nose reddened. The frequency of these episodes had lessened but every once in a while her eyes would flood and she would stop being able to talk.

I told her the gym teacher must have meant the other Sarah Lewis. A mistake. Because it had happened to Kevin, too, I said and shut up. I didn't want to tell her about that. Forgetting she was holding the spatula, she pushed her hair back. The plastic paddle poked her but, in her relief, Ma only smiled.

I was the one left disturbed. I sat on my bed with my knees up. If your mother doesn't have to worry about you, what kind of person are you?

Kevin's experience with the other Sarah Lewis was that some new kid told him his sister's face looked like raw meat. Kevin tried to tell him that that Sarah Lewis wasn't his sister but in the middle of his explanation to this jeering kid he was, he said, rocked by an equation. These books he was reading, they didn't have to be just words. If they were just words, then either 1.) they were for shit or 2.) he was a coward. He thought they were remarkable. Ergo, it followed—if he wasn't a coward, he could put them directly to work in his life, starting right then. He could institute his own karmic prevention policy.

"But what happened with that kid?" I asked.

"What kid?"

"The one who said my, I mean, Sarah's face looked like raw meat?"

"Oh," Kevin said. He couldn't hit him or anything because that also would incur negative karma and besides I might as well know that . . . He paused, head down. And he was going to have to tell Ma and Dad sooner or later, too, that . . . He did not finish this sentence either.

"What?"

Kevin rambled. He said he would not go so far as those guys who wore masks so they wouldn't murder bugs by inhaling them. He himself had no religious basis for his position at all, not even being a Quaker. He wasn't partial to silence; he liked to talk to most people, even strangers. He didn't know where he fit in. But still he didn't think he could hurt anybody. On purpose. Knowing in advance. Kevin said he was pretty sure his path was to refuse to harm living creatures. Not everybody's path, maybe. But his.

I didn't follow the masks or the Quakers, but as to Kevin not hurting anybody—this was no revelation. He'd always fled when Dad started talking about his bombing missions during the war. Unlike other sons in our neighborhood, my brother had never been interested in combat, no way, no how. The upshot of the encounter with this kid turned out to be that Kevin informed him about the eventual liability in such an unkind remark and the kid shoved him into a locker, banging the back of his head. Kevin had taken this painful blow as a sign. "An omen," he said darkly, "of wounds to come." My brother looked up from underneath long bangs. Of the two of us, he got the eyelashes—of course—the kind that hold points of water caught in them like dew.

Delton Jenkins' collision with Sarah Lewis occurred Homecoming Week. I could not understand the big deal about homecoming—no alumni returned to stroll the halls of Port Sabine High or poke around in its trophy case and we—the current crop—were already home. But there would be the game and the queen with her tiara and the dance and more butcher paper signs and gold and white crepe paper than usual. And we had an assembly in the auditorium. Sitting down front in their regular clothes, the band played. The cheerleaders jumped with one leg straight out and the other bent behind them and balanced on each others' shoulders, their pom poms like huge chrysanthemums. The football players stood up and got cheered for. Then the chorus mounted the stage in their black robes and filed up on the risers. Sarah Lewis was stationed in the back row because she was tall; Edward Fortner's coconut head was just below. Mrs. Peterson signaled to the pianist and faced the chorus, conducting. The flab above her elbows swung; her hands curlicued the finishes. For homecoming they sang familiar songs: "America the Beautiful" and "The Battle Hymn of the Republic"; Karen McManus did the solo there, a stratosphere soprano warbling like you'd hear Sundays at the Methodist church. Mrs. Peterson chose to end with "Cotton Fields," and she'd assigned that solo to Delton Jenkins.

I don't know what they'd practiced but I noticed the pianist had to slow herself down. Delton didn't make any rousing hand-clapper of it. He sang it as a lilting dirge. As his husky voice hovered and soared, the whole auditorium was seized with quiet. This should have been one of those rare times in high school when something out of the ordinary is offered and received to the benefit of all. It worked that way with me. For the first time I understood what people meant when they said someone had a gift: a thing that is not bought by effort or pain or humiliation or self-doubt, a thing that can't be taught. I felt wistfully jealous. I thought that if you had a gift, you were guaranteed that at least one part of your life would always be right. While the rest of the chorus provided a key-shifting drone for his voice to float over, Delton Jenkins just opened his mouth and allowed his talent to saturate the auditorium.

Sarah Lewis was placed beneath a stage light, illuminated from above. So were two other kids but it was her you saw. A harsh reflection pooled about her head, which drooped privately to one side. Sarah was not humming the background chords; she was mouthing the words along with Delton. Her face was rapt with admiration. She was gazing down on him like an angel in a Christmas card. As the song went on, her brow wrinkled and her head drooped further. It seemed to me that Sarah's angel was not announcing a baby's blessedness with rays of light. Her angel knew what the baby's end would be.

But I guess I was the only one to imagine that. Elbowed, I turned to see Linda Meyers imitating Sarah. Linda threw her head back, writhing in epileptic ecstasy, both hands on her chest as if her heart were thumping out of it. Laughter rippled. A few of the chorus glanced out but they couldn't determine what was happening, not from up there. By the time Mrs. Peterson turned around glaring, the laughter had spread and overtaken the rows all around Linda. Delton faltered at the finish. Not that he hit any wrong notes, just that he seemed to run out of them. He walked off the stage while people were still clapping. Mrs. Peterson waddled after him. The puzzled chorus followed, lumbering down the risers.

But it wasn't over yet. As the chorus milled around hanging up their robes, Sarah Lewis went over to Delton who was sitting in a chair in the chorus room like he didn't want to leave. She complimented him on how pretty he'd sung that song, and then she added, "I'm sorry y'all were slaves, Delton." That's what she said. I don't know who told but by the end of the day everybody knew about it. Some kids were indignant—like she'd blamed them somehow or spoken for them, too, when she sure as hell hadn't. Others giggled— Randy Fisher the science fair winner said maybe she could be sorry for the Crusades, while she was at it. All we heard about Delton was that his head went back. I wondered what he felt when Sarah said that; I wondered what all the colored kids felt about it but that remained a mystery. Nobody asked. My bet was that if Delton Jenkins had ever in his mind conceived of and pictured such an occasion—Had he? Somebody apologizing to him for enslaving his ancestors?—this was not the scene he would have invented. If it had been me, I'd have imagined big—a delegation with a golden scroll, an act of Congress, the knees of a nation going down. Not one white girl in a ratty choir robe.

The chorus got filled in, of course, as to why they'd been

laughed at. Interpretation was swift and merciless, and the word went out the same way: Sarah Lewis had a little white baby and now she wanted a little black one to go with it.

I could just hear Edward Fortner's wide, slitty mouth enlighten her: "They're saying you have a little white baby and now . . ." Who knows if he did. But Sarah couldn't have missed the looks and catcalls thrown her way. It was Friday before she dared to venture over to Cecile after school. Delton removed himself to the far fringe of the group. Cecile kept looking away from Sarah, in the direction of the others. As soon as the bus was in sight, she piled her books, got up off the ground and made for the sidewalk. But she was caught. Sarah had hold of her, brushing the dried grass from the back of her skirt. She squatted there burnishing the skirt like a pot or a mirror. Like Cecile was supposed to appreciate that. The bus turned into the drive and the rest of the kids headed toward it. Cecile looked frantic. Finally she jerked her hem out of Sarah's hands and ran to the bus. She ran like she would never come back. She jumbled in with the others at the bus steps, fit herself right into the middle of those kids, belonging to them and not Sarah.

I DID NOT want to go to the homecoming dance with Duffy Price because I'd already been to the movies with him once and he repeated the actors' lines to himself under his breath. Bonnie Parker said of an oldtimey car, "But we come in this one"; Clyde Barrow, stealing them another car, grinned, "That don't mean we have to go home in it." Duffy echoed ". . . go home in it," while I hugged the far armrest. I went to the dance with Duffy because though they charged both a couples' fee and a stag fee at the door, traditionally only boys went stag. A girl had to have a date. The colored kids had knocked the tradition a little; some of them came in a bunch, sitting in a block on the sideline folding chairs when they weren't dancing. You could dance with more people that way. I was supposed to dance only with Duffy. Mostly, I escaped from him.

The student council had hired a band from Houston; they had puffy Beatle hair and a keyboardist who played standing up. The lead tried to play his guitar over his head and lost his place in the music. Bass and drums thumped on without him until he recaptured the tune. A projector of sorts flashed the light show, now speckling the band, now drenching the dancers in a wash of purple or blue. There was no dialogue for Duffy to repeat here so he windmilled his arms while we danced or stood with his hands in his pockets. I drank a lot of pink punch and talked to whoever I could, even Miss Weisbach, even Kevin. It wasn't that we wanted to talk; it was that a gym isn't that huge and it got hard for us not to run into one another. Kevin didn't have on a tie or even a decent shirt, just a faded Banlon and a loose corduroy jacket of Dad's. What Kevin had was a date who wasn't a girl.

She was a woman—and not a particularly new one, either. Staring me down meaningfully, Kevin said, "This is Leslie. She works at the library. Leslie, this is my sister." Leslie wore glasses and a kind of limp party dress over black stockings. It was safe to say she was the only person at the 1967 homecoming dance with black stockings. I made a small wave in front of my chest and said "Hi." Leslie, who'd been extending her hand to shake mine, then took hers back and looked like she didn't know what to do with it. But she figured that out. She put it on Kevin.

Duffy hunted me down with more punch. I drank every last drop, feeling a leaden sorrow for myself—the restroom, with all the girls dropping wadded brown paper towels on the floor was more fun than out here. Meeting my brother's secret womanfriend was probably the high point of the dance for me—and it didn't have anything to do with me. But there was another, later, though I could not decide if it was high or low or anything more than that there was a point to it, definitely a point.

Around ten o'clock, I noticed some people packed together and wandered over there, threading around them, trying to see better. I figured a couple would be clowning around, doing an old-fashioned dance like the tango or the twist. Or somebody had spiked the punch with Everclear and was now staggering in an interesting way to the music. Only there wasn't a funny but an intent mood to the people crowded there. I heard a boy say "Whoa," and I stood on tiptoe, gripping his shoulder.

I'd never have thought she'd come to a dance, but there was Sarah Lewis in a spaghetti strap dress, dancing all by herself in the space carved out for her. She was barefooted. Her eyes, smudged underneath with black, were shut. Her whole face was shut, really, in what at first seemed a sullen cast. Resentful. And then I thought it was the kind of expression people have when they close their eyes and lips tightly waiting for a pain to pass.

The singer's voice dropped out leaving the band to an endless instrumental, drums driving behind the lead guitar. Sarah danced on the balls of her bare feet, heels just above the gym floor, and she wasn't fooling around— she was putting everything she had into it. Her long thighs worked. Her hips pumped, her dress wrenched and twisted at the waist. The spaghetti-straps slipped from her shoulders and strained against her upper arms as she raised them. Her long hair beat across her, hiding then showing, over and over, the bulge of her breasts above the scoop neckline. Miss Weisbach had called Sarah a problem-solver. She was solving a problem here, deliberately, that much I could tell from the set of her mouth. But I couldn't see into Sarah as on other occasions. She wasn't glass tonight. She was more like a prism flashing in the dark. The light show painted her face, arms, breasts, and her open palms a succession of colors. Sarah had never acted like a knowledgeable person but now she looked like she was flinging knowledge out from herself in reckless bursts of blue, purple, violent green.

Who she was flinging it at was anybody's guess. The semicircle I was crammed into was made up of white kids, some bright-eyed, others expressionless. The circle was completed by the spectator chairs where the colored kids congregated. Cecile Jenkins stood over there, next to another girl who had cocked her hip and folded her arms in front of her chest. The boys sat still as a jury. As if, feeling themselves observed, they wanted to be seen as impartial—and innocent, though gathered in a guilty place. Delton moved, finally—placed his hands between his knees and studied them.

Last chords slashed. The guitarist's arm had to be wheeling but I did not turn to watch him. Like everybody else's, my eyes were on Sarah. She stopped and the music fell away, and I swayed as though I'd stepped off a carnival ride and missed my footing. Sarah bent over, stumbling a little. The crowd flowed back from her. When she straightened, a pair of slingback heels dangled from one wrist like a bracelet. She thumbed up her straps but one fell off again as she passed through the circle. Sarah Lewis kept walking, across the floor, out the gym door, and out of our lives, though we didn't know it then, as we watched her cut that wake.

It was all over the halls, first thing Monday, and even in the teachers' lounge, I heard, where the consensus was the school was lucky it had Escaped Without Incident. The seat in front of me in English class was vacant. Molly Giles—she should have known better, she knew us both—grabbed me in the hall. "I heard about you," she said.

I stared at her. "About me what?"

"At that dance." She had a naughty sparkle in her eyes and a clear, snapping judgement. Whatever Sarah had meant by dancing like that, Molly didn't linger on the historical side of it or the hell-with-all-y'all side or even the lonely or hurt side. Molly chose to see the sexy side. A girl dancing. Boys watching. Uh huh.

"Not me." Slowly I shook my head.

I could see her realizing her obvious mistake. "Oh it was her." Molly walked backward down the hall. "Now you sure it wasn't you I heard about?" she called. By then she was just teasing. It came to me she was teasing all along.

Still, nobody had ever said that to me before, *I heard about you.*


MA WAS DABBING rouge when I got home, using a compact mirror. She licked her little finger and smoothed her eyebrows. She had to go meet my uncle, who'd called begging for a loan. Shutting the compact, she said she just might hang him out to dry. She hadn't decided yet because she had a more pressing matter on her mind: the mother-grapevine had informed her about the dance. I was wondering what I should say about Kevin but the mother-grapevine had truly swung past this one. All she wanted to know was that it was not me dancing in that . . . fashion she had heard about.

I made a face at her.

"I don't have to worry that you've turned into some kind of exhibitionist?"

"No." But I was worried now that I would never turn into anything.

"Thank God it wasn't you," Ma said. "Do you know about white women who display themselves to Negro men? Do you know what terrible things can happen?"

"Ma."

"No, I mean it. Actions—even ones you think are innocent—have consequences. It's time you realized that."

"But I don't have any actions." I meant this as a defense but the sound of it chilled my bones.

I would have to ask Kevin if in his books he had found a term for a person who went around siccing karma on everybody else, like that was their job. Because Sarah Lewis had done that—and if Kevin's books were right, in her next life she could be reborn beautiful and lucky. Linda Meyers would return as a rat. She would bite herself and die from rabies. As for me, I was in clear danger of having to live this life all over again—more, identical years of changing a grandma, hearing a brother's heels scrape the windowsill, watching a mother watch fish. I needed to locate, fast, a piece of me who could do even one of the things Sarah Lewis had done—get naked in the mud, drop out of school, have a baby, bury a husband—or get a second chance at school and mess that up, too.

That I had no actions seemed just fine to Ma. She reached over to pet my head. I flinched away like her tender hand would burn into my scalp if it fell on me, and she acted surprised, then hurt.

I tried to tell her how her definition of good wasn't so great for me, not at this point anyway. I tried to discuss like people do but it seemed we didn't have the knack. Ma was masochistically rifling Kevin's notebook for any fresh grades he might have brought home. She extracted a sheet of notebook paper and froze. "There's no such grade as F–, is there?" She angled the paper sideways to read a doodle in the margin. "And who is Leslie?"

Avoiding eye contact, I said I'd never heard of an F–.

"And? This girl is in one of his classes? Is she nice?"

I said she'd have to ask Kevin about that.

"He never tells me anything." Ma sat down on the couch and let her head fall back.

Grandma inched through the living room, making her way by grasping a chair top, the couch arm, the breakfast bar. We could hear her knocking around in the kitchen. "Fed the fish," she said as she crept past us again. We saw the back of her housedress, wet, the pink primroses darkened. We smelled her.

Ma stared at some high, distant point on the living room wall. Her soul removed itself from her body and hung nearby, patient as a sweater. My mother looked like she had picked an innocent star to wish on and that star had turned out to be a planet. Now the planet was advancing toward her in colossal mass. It was hurtling closer and closer blinding her with its speed and she could not get out of its way. Just before it pulverized her, her soul slid back in and she blinked, glanced at her watch, heaved herself up from the couch, and strode down the hall to my brother's room.

Ma looked bare-faced when she came back, like the rouge had evaporated from her skin. She told me Kevin had work to do. He had to write that paper over and persuade his teacher to take it. She didn't care if he had to wash the teacher's feet with his hair. I also had work to do. I had to make Grandma put on a clean dress and underwear. Then— my mother focused on the inside of her purse, she raked around without looking at me—she said to call the nursing homes and make a list of each one's amenities—

"Amenities?"

"Okay, features," she said, what nice features the homes offered, what size rooms and recreation and nursing care they had and what kind of food they served, and how much each one cost.

"Not really, Ma."

She got a lipstick out of her purse, ran it around her lips and threw it back in the purse. She shouldered into her coat. "Oh really," she said.


THERE WAS THANKSGIVING and there was Christmas, then we were in the car parked at a curb.

Grandma clutched a paper bag Kevin had given her. I

knew only one item that was in it; I had no idea what else he'd included. Maybe a sandwich. Maybe carrying the bag made Grandma feel better. Carrying the suitcases made me feel awful. Grandma was already alarmed, her pupils darting in fear. Dad lifted her out of the car. As we started up the steps of the place, Ma and Dad supporting her elbows, she sagged back. She asked was Papa here.

"He is *not*," Ma said. Dad looked sick and like he wanted to belt Ma. Ma kept wiping the corners of her mouth with a kleenex that became a smaller and smaller ball. She said to leave the suitcases at reception, and Grandma and I should go on in and explore. There were lots of pleasant spaces here. Grandma and I left them folded over in the office, both of them with their reading glasses on, signing all the forms.

You couldn't walk slowly enough to keep up with Grandma; you encountered forced periods of stasis and contemplation. As we crept the perimeter, we passed a lounge with card tables and beige vinyl chairs, the kind that urine or worse can be wiped off of. A Christmas tree—lights unplugged—dripped silver icicles on a cabinet television. We passed a room with naked legs on a bed, shapeless ones square over the hunk of kneebone. A spidery person—all arms and abdomen—was wheeled past us. Eventually we hit the dining hall, row after row of long formica slabs, wiped for lunch. An old man already lurked at a table. Once he saw we weren't bringing food trays, he stopped seeing us.

There, over in the corner, under a picture made from glued beans and corn, glowed an aquarium on a metal stand. It was lit from inside and busy with flickering, a small watery green fair.

We took some time to get there. Me on one side and on the other, Grandma patting the white walls for balance or grasping the window casings as we made our way. I brought a couple of metal folding chairs over so we could sit by the aquarium. Why didn't they have padded chairs in this room, too? There were probably fifty butts here with as little flesh cover as Grandma's. She watched the fish but she wasn't happy about it.

"You wanna talk?" I asked her.

She nodded Yes.

"Want to say something?"

She shook her head No.

"Want me to?"

"Yeah," she said. After a long concave slide of chest wall, her stomach and her breasts merged together, *lump lump*; the paper bag rested on her stomach. Maybe it contained her bedsore ointment. No, Kevin disdained utility; he favored the spiritual gift.

I could have told her about a girl who came back to school with my name and affected my life in a way I wished I didn't have to understand. She would listen but she wouldn't like that story. Nothing much happened—some talking and a dance. Grandma liked stories with the threat of destruction, with adventure and rescues and magic animals. Her eyes would follow you then. So I told her the story of Buddy Lewis, which more or less fit her specifications. Because what was Buddy Lewis if he wasn't a magic animal? What did it matter if she thought Vietnam was a sawmill town in Polk County? She just wanted to be surrounded by a voice she knew.

I was planning to tell her Buddy moved into a room with yellow paint and a chenille bedspread and that room was in a house with new friends and he was happy there and safe, very safe. But then I saw myself, Sarah Lewis, walking out of this place and leaving Grandma and her suitcases behind and looking at her face as I left her there—because in a little while that's what I would do. So, keeping my voice gentle, I told her all about Buddy, who'd had a gift as surely as Delton did, a gift that didn't save him—and I ended the story the way Sam Maynard had, with a heavy fall through air, a rushing up of ground. Not on the rational surface maybe, but down deep, Grandma was a stone expert on that.

Then we sat there. Ma and Dad must have been on their twentieth form. It occurred to me I could crash a folding chair through the window. Not that I would, but that I could.

I opened Grandma's paper bag and took out the cylinder of fish food. The nursing home people had been happy to accept our donation. Kevin, my accomplice, had smiled over the karmic implications of the plan. The aquarium deal—a theft from Ma which traded out to be a provision for Grandma—was my idea. Plainly it was not much, but it was not quite nothing, either. There would be consequences.

"Grandma, look what's here." I rattled the paper sack.

Also in there were a tangerine—good, Kevin, an apple would have been too hard for her—a row of sugar cookies bulged in a baggie, and some peace stickers Grandma could press on the furniture in her new room. "Look," I said. I twisted the top and handed her the fish food. With me practically lifting her, she stood up to sprinkle the flakes. Those fish were trained. They rose, open-mouthed as singers, just at the shadow of her trembling hand.

# Vidor

MR. CHARLES got this idea that for the last game the drums should wear capes but the drums balk. The rest of the band marches formations as he threatens them into their costumes. Sulkily the drums predict: if there's any wind they'll get wound up in the capes and have to fight their way out. Does Mr. Charles want the school board to see that performance? The band director clenches his jaw. Then he feels a tapping on his shoulder and wheels glaring to find Della Jefferson, a clarinet. She reminds him that the band at her old school— the Negro high school—all wore capes. Smiling, she offers to demonstrate. "Oh please do," Mr. Charles sighs and Della spins herself into the cape. "It's fun, y'all," she promises—a little shyly—the row of suspicious eyes. "Everybody'll be watching y'all." Della plays the Look Sharp march, doing half-turns while the cape swirls behind her, shaking her own rhythm into the air. When she full-turns she might as well have a pair of wings. The drums' eyes—even Evvie Budinger's who is distracted today—light up. One of them grabs Della and capes flying, they all rush out to the poor laggers on the field and with a burst of drumming become the band again. When Mr. Charles blows his whistle, they fall out and lie on the ground like they've all been shot. "How amazingly funny," Mr. Charles frowns but he will probably let them go soon; the white November sky is growing pink. Way across the field the football team is still hitting each other.

Evvie Budinger sits crosslegged, uprooting fistfuls of dried grass. She's contemplating a problem—sex with her boyfriend Rennie—but her thoughts are interrupted by her brother Mason's voice, saying "Yeah?" and "No kidding" and "What do you think you want to do?" In the intervals some softer voice, rising in a question. "No, that would be a cinch for you," Mason says with conviction. A rush of murmuring in response, flutelike. "Believe it," Mason says.

Evvie cranes around; yep, he's talking to just who she thought he was. Mason is angled away from her so she can't see the one renegade front tooth that overlaps the other, or the patience in his thin face, the enthusiasm that pours out from her brother like traceable streams of light. Even lying down, he still seems to be bending to listen. Mason always does that, he grew to 6'2" at thirteen and now at 17 he's already a little stooped. He doesn't weigh nearly enough.

 Mason is talking about what it's like to be drum major. He's describing how the first game, he ran through the band then pivoted and faced them. Threw his baton high in the air and caught it. He loved it when the people went crazy. They didn't expect him to catch it; all Port Sabine High School drum majors before him dropped the baton. But Mason caught it and started off and "the whole band just swept along behind me."

Evvie raises her voice. "We're supposed to follow you, Mase. We practice that."

The back of Mason's hand waves her off. "That green field," he says, "opened out like a prairie."

Mason truly feels all this about the band. He took Latin for the second year because he didn't want to hurt poor Mr. Flynn's feelings (his wife died last summer)—if no one takes Latin Mr. Flynn could be out of a job. Mason reads all the time, all those books their teachers tell them to read; he even borrowed Evvie's *Art of the Ancient World* book.

He has not returned it.

"Yeah me, too," Mason says. "For the rest of my life. I wish it wasn't the last game already. I'd like to throw the baton up a few more times. Grab it out of the air."

Mr. Charles blows the whistle; the piccolo groans, the tubas snore.

On the other side of the field one football player stands apart, hands on his hips, staring toward the band. From this distance he couldn't pick out who is who; the whole band is just a lot of bodies on the ground. That's just as well. Because Evvie has a hunch that it is Attis Fuller looking this way. Della and Attis, late of G.W. Carver, are colored members of Port Sabine High's first integrated senior class. And Mason, her dumb white brother, the finest person Evvie knows, is pouring out his heart to Della Jefferson.

"I step off out there and it's like the world fans out behind me." Mason stands up and brushes off the dried grass, gives a hand to Della. A beautiful girl with a face the color of dusk, she leaps up holding her clarinet.

"The world moves when I do and when I wave my hands it makes music, and me and everybody else in the world weave in and around each other making music," Mason says. "Isn't that how it is?"

SINCE THE LAST game of the '68 season is against Vidor, the coach is tortured by politics. Port Sabine has colored players now, and they may not want to go to Vidor. Or maybe they do. Or it may be their daddies and mamas won't want them to go. After practice he engineers it so Wayne Flowers the team manager asks them. "Don't make nothing big of it, hear?" Coach warns Wayne. But it turns into a thing.

If anybody else had asked them it might have been a fight but at 17 Wayne Flowers's vocation is pretty well set and known; he will be a priest. Last spring alone in his room he let himself say it *Pax vobiscum*; the counterblessing surged back, sounding his solid body like a chord. Wayne shoulders the water cooler and seeks them out—Attis and Albert and Fast Paul, who really is fast, and Richard, who all the other colored guys call Ricky Dick but none of the white guys do. But since they've heard him called that, they think it, so he's Ricky Dick to them, too. "Y'all want to go to Vidor?" Wayne asks them.

That little Texas town east of Port Sabine has an oak tree carved with the words *Nigger don't let the sun set on you in Vidor.*

"Naw," Richard says but Attis nails him with a slit-eyed look.

"Whyn't you say what's on your mind."

Attis is not all that used to talking to white people but he steps up to Wayne. Attis's brother in California says things are happening in this country in this sad, bad year. Things are rising, my little brother, he's promised Attis.

Wayne told no one about the event in his room but it has settled into his eyes as a stillness. He shrugs, "Just thought maybe y'all didn't want to go."

Attis shoots back, "Right on with you there." Fast Paul and Albert echo *Right on.* Wayne isn't sure what this means but he understands they've agreed with him.

He nods to the coach but the coach makes signals with his eyebrows. Wayne sighs, setting down the cooler.

"Listen, coach, maybe the colored guys shouldn't go this Friday."

Coach starts to look around and then Attis Fuller says Black and Coach says What? and Attis says, "The black players don't want to go to Vidor."

Gravely, Coach stows his clipboard under his arm and rests his fists in his sweatshirt pockets. "What y'all white players think of that?" Heads turn in the dusk. The white boys grew up here. They all know about the tree. They can walk a mile in those moccasins, they say All right.

"But the black players gone go to Vidor."

Coach and Ricky Dick and everybody else looks at Attis. Wayne says, "Don't want none a y'all to get hurt."

Rennie Thibodeaux the quarterback wipes his forehead with the belly part of his jersey. "Hell, Father Wayne, you tell me how those candyasses gonna hurt us."

Someone else growls Yeah and then Fast Paul's fist strikes the air and Attis Fuller grins at him and the whole team is whistling and stomping the practice field.


WRAPPED UP in her cape, Evvie waits on the hood of Rennie's Ford until he's finished with his shower. She wants to show him her new painting. Miss Janes the art teacher has called it "powerful," the first encouragement Evvie has ever received, aside from Mason's. One star, then another, pokes through the deepening blue.

Evvie is afraid she is not smart enough to be a painter because she is so often felled by questions. For instance. She got booed by a whole class when they debated "America: Love it or Leave it" and Evvie blurted out why did it have to be just two things? Wasn't there like some other thing that could happen? Another for instance. Evvie's parents have told her sex without marriage is wrong but Evvie's experience has not verified this. The real problem, as she sees it, had not been brought to her attention at all: falseness. Both her lives—art class, band, Mason . . . and her body with Rennie's—are exactly real. But because she has to keep one life secret, in the other she has become an imposter. Evvie Budinger, 16, rests her worried head in her hands and tells herself she wants to be not innocent and not confused.

When Rennie comes out with his gym bag, Evvie drags him down the hall, his hair wet, his shirt still sticking to his shoulders in dime-sized spots. She flips on the light to all the colors of the art room. Rennie complains of the glare but he sets down the gym bag, slides his hands in his pockets and peers at the painting Evvie did of Mason.

"Why are there all those white streaks?"

"But that's how Mason is." Evvie is surprised. "You know Mason."

"Not with white stripes on him." Rennie sees Evvie's face. "But it's good. No, really, Eveline, it's good."

"You tell little kids good."

When Rennie positions himself by the back windows more of Mason Budinger's homely face shines from the wall. Rennie makes some clicking noises with his tongue while he thinks it out. "He looks like it's Christmas Day," he finally says.

"Thank you." Evvie smiles and she can see he's relieved, pondering the success of his remark.

They go by his house first, of course, because his mom is dead and his dad works nights and every place in the house is theirs. Barely through the front door Rennie Thibodeaux runs a finger along her ribs and Evvie Budinger applies her entire self up against his entire self. They lose their breaths. They start stepping on clothes. An inner material of gold sparkles swells and bursts all along the filigree net of their skin. When Rennie has it on he lifts her, her legs hooking round him, her arms holding on and on and on. By the end they're both yelling and they tumble over onto the couch and look at each other with a pure wonder at what they can make with themselves.

Rennie wants to know exactly why he was right about Mason's picture. Evvie's index finger traces his jaw. During the "America: Love it or Leave it" discussion, they had been confounded to realize they were not on the same side. Worse—after Eleanor Pennimore said: "We have an obligation beyond ourselves . . . to our country," Rennie swiveled round to nod at Eleanor's exalted face. Now Evvie has an awful thought.

"Eveline."

"What? Oh." She explains, as he asked, the idea behind her painting: that those white stripes are just color representations of the kind of fervor that comes out of Mason. Rennie listens then kisses her just below the ear.

At home, Evvie wanders into Mason's room. He has her *Art of the Ancient World* book open. "I am so willing," Mason stares at a page of slim, sloe-eyed, side-walking Egyptian women, "to be broadened by education." Evvie pinches his skinny bicep and says he needs to be a lot broader.

Mason shakes his head sadly. "That is not a clever answer."

"So I'm not a clever person." Evvie's brow furrows.

Mason just looks at her. "You liar," he says.

He opens *Art of the Ancient World* again, to a page with the corner turned down. They gaze at a copper-faced woman with black hair, a tiny waist, and bare little breasts.

What makes her like she is, for all time? Good paint, Evvie supposes and desert air, beauty and boldness. And what makes Della like she is? Beauty—bright, wide eyes, skin not copper but caramel-gold shadowed with rose and violet. Is Della bold? Della's part of everything, Evvie decides, because she never thinks she isn't part.

Evvie leans over and gently thumps her brother's forehead. "Look, Mase, about this crush on—"

"Shut up," he whispers. He holds up the book in both hands. The Egyptian woman's feet walk sideways but she has turned her face straight on to Mason's. "I want to live up to you," he tells her.

Then he turns the light of his gaze on Evvie. His eyes are a different brown than she has seen before. Mason reaches up and tugs at a tangle in her hair. "So how's Rennie-tin-tin?"

Evvie jerks away. She can't bear to reveal what she thought earlier: that Rennie Thibodeaux is going to marry a girl who can say out loud just what he feels inside, and that girl is not her. Neither can she tell her brother how sometime in the night the faint blue ovals of Rennie's fingerprints will appear on her skin. She can't say, Look. Isn't it a mystery?

MASON TOOK LATIN II because he likes Mr. Flynn. Also because he feels sorry for him: the neighbors blabbed to everyone how one day last summer Mr. Flynn rambled around the back yard calling his dead wife's name.

Only four kids signed up for Latin, but five are here today. Mr. Flynn is operating at a shade above a whisper. He speaks gently and very very softly so that Bobby McLenehan, left over from basic math, does not wake up. Mr. Flynn writes on the board Julius Caesar's message to the Senate: Veni, vidi, vici. When he makes them repeat it, he pushes air down with his hands so they understand to keep their voices low. McLenehan's cheek is glued to the desk with drool, his mouth wide open; every so often his free hand jerks.

Attis Fuller knows him from the football team where McLenehan plays tight end or would play tight end if the entire team including Father Flowers the waterboy were assassinated and only McLenehan were left. Attis looks at the sorry spectacle and rubs his forehead. He hated Latin I but kept on because of Della Jefferson. The first day of school as the G.W. Carver kids filed in, a white woman hollered at them. Attis knew to just keep his head up and walk on but Della, clutching a notebook to her chest, stopped and looked at her. It seemed to Attis that what the white woman was yelling got slowed down in her mouth. He still does not know how to say what was on Della's face.

Della is the only one in the class besides Mr. Flynn who doesn't think of Latin as dead. She likes the puzzle of it, the way you slip off one ending and fit on another to make the sentence right, and she appreciates its silent power, its presence in stone. Once in a dream, Della's mother fed her a platter of biscuits; furled in the center of each was a Latin word. Della spit them from her mouth and built a pile of curly scrolls.

Sue Childers, Latin II's fourth legitimate student, smiles at McLenehan and rips a strip of paper from the notebook page she has titled Julius Caesarhead and His Pukey Wars.

74

When Mr. Flynn turns his back to write on the board, she lofts her spitball but misses Bobby's open mouth; it bounces off his cheek. One of his shoulders twitches.

The class unites, intent. When Mr. Flynn turns around, he smiles at the alert postures, the sudden attention to their books. He directs them to a paragraph at the bottom of page 47. They read it together aloud quietly. The next time Mr. Flynn adjusts his glasses and peers down, three spitballs fly toward Bobby. Two plink soundlessly against the desk and slide to the floor but the other connects with his earlobe.

Attis mouths *Rim shot* and Mason falls over his desk holding his ribs. He motions for Attis to tell the others but Attis draws back into himself, bashful, so Mason scribbles a note and holds it up: Rim shot. Trying to muffle her laugh, Sue snorts.

Then they all look more or less straight front and whisper, Veni vidi vici, making the v's into w's: I came, I saw, I conquered.

Describing the life of a Roman foot soldier, Mr. Flynn treads softly through the aisles to the back of the class. Sue lobs a beauty this time; all eyes follow its trajectory toward the goal, McLenehan's slack mouth. And then the spitball disappears into a hand from nowhere.

"Vidi," Mr. Flynn smiles: I saw.

When the bell rings Bobby McLenehan jumps up from the desk like it's a fire drill and tries to run in two directions at once. Blinking, he glares around then jams his books high up under his arm and strides out.

Attis and Mason stand in the hall on either side of Della, laughing. Della's hand covers her mouth. After Bobby is far enough away, she takes it off laughing aloud, her head thrown back. She is, Mason calculates, beyond any Egyptian tomb painting. The color of some beautiful sunset land, Della is her own country. Her descending hand falls onto Mason. Mason knows she's not even thinking. Her hand on his forearm means nothing. Nevertheless he says to himself, *She is touching my body*. Some distant part of him not governed by joy notices that Attis Fuller has stopped laughing.


MASON SHOWS EVVIE a note he'd pushed over to Della and one she's written back. In Latin. Every once in a while, he says, Mr. Flynn stops his declension and taps his pen on the lectern. "If I could, Miss Jefferson, just direct your considerable powers to the ablative case, we might do great things." He smiles with a kind of mutual pleasure. Mason says he's joking but not meanly at them. He's joking with some private audience inside himself. It's like he's not alone in there.

Mason folds the note back into one of the plastic photo squares in his wallet. "I'm going to tell you something."

Evvie cocks her head.

"Swear you won't tell."

"Tell what?"

"I wouldn't want anybody to know because I like him. And not Mom and Dad because they're not various-minded enough. But you are."

"Various-minded? What is that?"

Mason's eyes soften. "Shut up. Mr. Flynn is just a little bit crazy."

The light still pours from her brother's face. Evvie relaxes; whatever he knows, he likes it. "Like how much?"

"Oh like 7 percent. Maybe 10."

"How do you know?"

Mason shrugs. "I just know. The weird thing is he really means that stuff about 'great things.'"

Mr. Flynn distributes a mimeograph and by the end of class Attis and Sue and Mason and Della have managed to translate the story of Horatio, who "caught all the javelins on his shield, and resolute as ever, stood on the bridge and held his ground." *Man* escapes Attis's mouth. Mr. Flynn steps back beaming. He almost pops his uncapped fountain pen into his white breast pocket. Attis points his finger just in time.

Mr. Flynn, the only PhD in classics who ever taught at Port Sabine High or ever will, has a great amount of money in several funds he never thinks about. He lived for nine years with a woman who had cancer. She kept getting new and different kinds. But every day they lived together they married each other again, the ceremony sometimes stealing over them, a surprise. They did have bad times—once Mr. Flynn came home early and found his wife on their bed with a pistol to her temple. He ran and got his service revolver from the war, stood in front of her and pressed it to his head. They looked at each other, both with gun barrels stuck to their heads. *You take all the drama out of it, Michael*, his wife said. When she died he drove to Taylor's bayou, rented a dinghy with an outboard, and putted to where a willow hung down. This time he slid the gun in his mouth. Then a snake S-curled the water and the pattern reminded him of the scallopped supports of Roman aquaducts, and the scallopped supports of the straight troughs above and those of the deep marks chariot wheels cut in the stone streets of Pompeii, and Pompeii of living people—women baking, women washing, cloth drifting on the surface of the water. Looking up through the green light of the late afternoon, he saw his Anne in a slender craft, a pirogue, he thought, loaded with burnished jars. Mr. Flynn knew at once that those jars held her scarred and radiant soul. She waved to him. He shook his hand free of the gun, sent it splashing into the bayou so he could wave back. He was as soothed as if her breath had entered his mouth. At sunset when the brown water ran red and gold and the mosquitos were about to eat him he took the boat in. Then Mr. Flynn drove home. It was a rare night—a heavy brass moon with the profile of Justinian stamped clear upon it, the sky royal purple above the refinery lights. He could still taste metal on his tongue.

AFTER THURSDAY'S BAND practice, Mason, carrying his whistle and his baton, is the last one to desert the field. Though they were tools only minutes ago, the whistle and baton are already becoming souvenirs. They make him sad, like a laughing snapshot of someone now dead. He could keep them to look at later—Evvie once showed him a painting of old boots and said you could find the boot-owner's life in them—but Mason doesn't see the point. He knows he will return the baton and whistle for next year's drum major. It seems purer to keep only what he's felt out here.

The team is trailing off the field now, too, and Attis Fuller, in dirty practice whites, lugging his helmet, crosses Mason's path. Attis has started to let his hair grow and it's got mashed places from the helmet.

"Budinger."

Attis uses Mason's last name for the formality of the occasion. He is angry he should have to put himself in such a position. He wishes Mason were a big chunk white boy but he looks like a tall old wilted celery stick with one mother tooth in front. Then he remembers Della's smiling at this celery stalk so easy and when she looks at Attis her mouth runs in one straight line.

"Don't talk to her no more."

Mason doesn't even ask who he is not supposed to talk to. He doesn't, as Attis hoped, go stiff-jawed with offense, so the encounter can be contained in a properly few words. He ruins it. Mason stoops toward him as though to listen more closely and asks, "Why not?"

"She ain't your business, you hear."

"Why not?"

Attis feels like his head bulges out with the pressure of the reasons why not. Della is not only the girl he loves but someone more belonging to him than Mason can ever understand. "You cain't even know why not," Attis assures Mason. "Cain't even start to."

"You mean because I'm white. I don't like Della because

78

she's colored—"

"Black."

"Okay, black. I like her because Della's someone. Already she is."

"And she pretty."

"Is that why you like her?"

Attis bangs his helmet against his leg. "You think I'm simple? Hear me what I'm sayin—you messin out of your business." It's not that colored has to stay with colored because of a law like in the old days. This is 1968—it's different now. Now the black man stands for himself, stands for the black woman and she for him, and this alliance is charged with a new-claimed and powerful beauty built atop depthless grief and shame. The vision fills Attis's eyes with fierce tears.

"The times has changed, Budinger."

Mason squints; what little Attis has said sounds backwards to him. Black people get served at the Holiday Inn now right in Port Sabine. White people linked arms in that march on Washington; Mason saw them on tv. He stoops a little further toward Attis.

"But you're talking like old times. People have a right to be friends with who they want to now."

"What you tell me about rights."

Mason's head bows. "Forget rights. It's personal."

This Attis does not want to hear. It seems to him that the events of this year transcend the personal; it seems to him now that his life will transcend the personal. He will fight, yes, whether he wins or not, Attis Fuller will fight. And maybe now, after all. He squints back at Mason.

"You think this black woman like you back?"

"Probably not the way I hope."

Attis's lips barely move. "Just what you hope?"

Mason forces himself to look into Attis's eyes—glittery in the sinking sun—for as long as he can. "The same thing as you, I guess."

"Aw, man!" Attis throws down his helmet. "You get to

79

like who wants you to like them. You don't go up to nobody and say Okay you like me now. And they just like you. It don't work that way!" This rushes out of Attis's mouth; he has not meant to say it. Saying it distracts him from his more profound and truer vision, and he rubs his throbbing forehead.

"I know they don't just like you. Look at me, Attis, you think I don't know that?"

Attis frowns. His head is pounding now. He scoops up his helmet and warns, "I done told you." His cleats scrape and clack on the parking lot.


FRIDAY EVENING, Della sits right up front across from the driver, beside another clarinet. Mason, bearing his relics almost at arm's length—baton and whistle and tall hat—makes his way back to the bus's last bench, installing his hat in the seat beside him. This is not out of fear of Attis though Attis could clearly demolish him in a fight. It is out of sadness and out of some sad sense he suspects lurks behind the nonsense of their talk.

"Look," Mason points with his baton out the window and Evvie, watching for the tree, scoots over to peer out. It's only Mr. Flynn waving to the band from his squatty Corvair. "You'll make me miss it!" she scolds Mason; by now everybody is on the lookout for the tree. They are pretty sure it will grow just by the Vidor City Limits sign. They have all driven this way a hundred times in their lives and never seen such a thing but maybe they haven't looked in the right place.

Later someone says *So maybe it's downtown by the courthouse or by the post office* and the band agrees to this probable central location. They think of the oak as Vidor: moss-green and hard and living. They imagine the carving growing inward as the tree grows. In twenty-five years an African-American man will try to live there in a federal housing project. A white man rings his doorbell to argue with him over whether

God is black or white. The black man lowers his head and touches his own hair. *You mean God's hair don't feel like that?*

On the way over Coach tries to get the team to sing. They've gone through the fight song once or twice then Coach rumbles into You Are My Sunshine and some of the players burst out laughing. In the middle of the bus where Fast Paul is sitting on the inside seat away from the window next to Bobby McLenehan, Bobby begins to emit guitar sounds then sawing guitar chords and he nudges Fast Paul. Fast Paul elbows him back. Bobby launches Purple Haze anyway, keeping it low. Attis and Albert and Richard, also assigned inside seats away from the windows, don't join in but their derisive grins inflame Bobby. At the song's end, all discretion escapes him. Bobby McLenehan yells *Scuse me while I kiss the sky*, jumps into the aisle and with crashing sound effects smashes one electric guitar on the rubber-mat bus floor. He smashes two or three more on Fast Paul who flinches away from the blows, protecting his head with both hands and snickering.

Coach bellows, "Goddamnit McLenehan get out of my sight, you're benched."

"News flash," Bobby mutters. He slides down into his seat, grinding his fists in his eyes. "Waaaaa, not for the whole game, Coach?"

"For infinity," Coach says, "now shut the hell up and concentrate your minds and your behinds on winning this game tonight." As the buses pull up in the high school parking lot, it is still light, one of those November sunsets when the sky is pink and blue like baby colors.

The team kneels on one knee in the oyster shell and Wayne Flowers leads them in a prayer. Holding the first aid kit, he says Let us be strong tonight. Let Jesus guide us—our legs and our eyes and our hands and may the way be clear. Help us play fair and if temptation arises, let us make it into the Ways of the Lord. When Wayne has been a priest for eleven years a woman in the door of a carnival trailer calls to him. He is not wearing his collar—she can't know what he is. He turns toward the sadness in her voice from years of habitually turning toward voices. Knowing he will go, that the price of the promise he is breaking, to her and to himself, will be years of arid service. Not knowing that as he holds her he will pretend it is some spring evening, that she is the wife he can touch and talk to. Not knowing that one day the brightness will fill him again and this night will be another separate brightness then.

Give us victory tonight if it is your will for we are bound always by that. In your name we pray. Amen.


AT HALFTIME, thanks to a fumble and a pass Rennie drilled into the stomach of a Vidor defensive back, Vidor is two up on them 14-0. Coach clumps around the locker room not making eye contact, nodding his head though no one has said anything. With a horrible patience, he sets his heavy foot up on a bench and leans an elbow on his knee. There is a knell in the long silence.

"Listen here, boys, football is a simple game." He offers them his big empty hands. "You cain't turn the football over."

The band has formed up in the end zone. Mason cannot help picking out Della's straight back as he runs through the ranks. For the last time. The band members' excited faces, when he wheels to them, seem dear, as though he can in one flash inhale the essence of each person. Even Evvie. His sister poises her sticks above the drum, jaw set but her face perplexed and dreamy. She looks to him then and tips a drumstick; he sees she's caught him postponing the moment as long as he can. Then the faces blur and to Mason the band is not a group of people but one bright agile beauty which marches over any land, piping and tooting and drumming any rhythm or tune, its front striding along elbows high, the rear twirling little circles then hopping back into step, all its pieces loving itself. The lights dazzle Mason's eyes. Mr. Charles paces down the sidelines. Mason throws his baton; it tumbles against the dark sky and falls back into his hand like a silver wish. The band bursts into music and follows him onto the field.

At the end of halftime, the band and the cheerleaders and a few zealot parents line up near the gate; the band plays the fight song as the team rushes back on. On the other side of the chain link, Mr. Flynn, muffled against the November chill, salutes the players with a cherry snow cone.

The coach hunches over his small blackboard drawing plays and snapping chalk. Late third quarter Vidor takes the kick and the receiver nursing the ball into the end zone has it jump up and bite him on the shin. Fast Paul snatches it away, raising it high in the end zone, but Anthony Fertitta's point-after kick arcs up and down like a sad pop fly. 14-6. Port Sabine manages to sit on Vidor for the next four downs and on second and ten, Rennie fades back searching for receivers Jimmy Culpepper and Attis Fuller who are buried, and finally locates *Thank you Jesus* Fast Paul who has slithered past a Vidor safety hearing him go *Oh shit* into unobstructed green. Excited, Rennie messes up and throws long; he's smacking his own helmet when Fast Paul sprouts wings and catches the ball. Touchdown. This time the kick, aided by a deadly curse from Anthony's Sicilian grandfather, clears the bar. Port Sabine stands roar. 14-13.

Seven minutes into the fourth quarter Fast Paul is tightroping down the Vidor sideline when a linebacker pushes him out of bounds; before he can turn to surrender the ball the guy knocks him down and plows him under. After lying flat on the cold grass with the stadium lights haloing and Coach flashing fingers in his face, he is helped out of the game by a clench-jawed Attis Fuller and Bobby McLenehan. Bobby has charged out on the field to menace the offender, changed his mind, and started for a referee. Coach, who cannot publicly strangle a player, wards off a penalty which would set his offense somewhere east of the Louisiana state line by snagging McLenehan to sling Fast Paul's arm over his shoulder and help walk him in.

By now Nigger this and Niggerlover that are coming pretty regularly from the Vidor line, and some of Port Sabine's players though they use these words themselves have had a strange feeling seize them, a feeling of Us and Them and the Us is clear and changed from any Us they have known before. This benefits Bobby McLenehan who in ten months will not have to do much prep work when an exasperated black sergeant hits him in the face during basic to get his attention. He will follow this man until their tour is over. When they are cut loose in San Francisco airport the sergeant brushes Bobby's shoulder and says *Hey man* and Bobby says it back, *Hey man nobody but you kept my ass a-live.*

Getting up from a pile, a stump-thick tackle bears down on Rennie Thibodeaux's instep and Rennie will later remember an auditory hallucination of fried quail bones cracking. Vidor intercepts his next wobbly pass and runs it all the way back. But on the extra point the football bonks against the post and bounces back to Port Sabine sidelines. No good. Coach, who's thrown down his balled-up towel, jerks it up again, his heart adip and aflutter with possiblity. And then with 20-13 Vidor and 1:17 to go Rennie limps back and finding Attis open sets the ball directly into his hands. Attis takes an instant hit to his left shoulder but keeps his feet and spins out of it. Grimacing, brow furrowed, he covers thirty populated yards, and the grand vision he has imagined in this situation, some whirl of righteous black power which is himself churning down history, does not come. Attis simply avoids shadow and form and penetrates green space. Touchdown. As the scoreboard changes to 20-19, the Port Sabine bleachers rise with his name.

Rennie looks to Coach for the signal and sure enough Coach, body strained forward like a bulldog on a mighty leash, thumps his left shoulder and doubles his fist. Rennie nods into the huddle, All right y'all, yeeha. He fakes a handoff to Jimmy Culpepper—poor Jimmy fakes out one fat guard—and ends up being chased. Rennie's arm is cocking—he's got to flatout throw now instead of toss to Richard, who is jumping up and down near the two, his hands curved and waiting. Half the Vidor defense is headed Richard's way; Coach has slapped the towel over his eyes. Rennie lets go and like he tells it in the locker room ten minutes later This fine man Ricky Dick manages to land the ball a quarter inch past goal with four linemen riding his shoulders. Richard, his eyes shining, likes hearing that so much he doesn't say Don't call me that, he says How many riding on me? so Rennie can say Six and then after some yelling Wayne Flowers mildly repeats How many? so Rennie says Eight and then Forty-two and pretty soon Richard has crossed the line with the whole town of Vidor on his back.

Coach strides around the wet floor grinning, lightly punching all the players and dodging punches in return; he lives for nights like this. But he recalls himself and hustles his players out to the bus.

The Port Sabine side has gone wild, bleachers rocking, the cheerleaders flipping, fathers slapping each other's backs, the band waving clarinets and horns and drumsticks and jumping and hugging each other. And Della Jefferson hugs Pam Wheatley and Karen Smith and Pattie Sievers and then she hugs Mason Budinger and Mason puts his long arms around her and kisses her.

USUALLY THE BAND whizzes off before the team but tonight the football bus is the one loaded up and idling. Smoking the end of a cigarette, Coach fills the bus door, studying the parking lot. A few men wait around in the oyster shell. The band walks by squeaking and tooting and going drum-a-thum-thum with their sticks to the players on the other side of their bus windows. The team cheers back. These men the coach studies may be just about to get in their cars and go home.

Mr. Charles accompanies Della Jefferson. She hugs her clarinet longways to her chest. They walk to the bus headdown and Mr. Charles, pausing for Della to climb on before him, angles to check the men and hears coach bark out something as a rock smashes a player's window. The football bus door slams; players' faces disappear from the windows. Some more rocks hit; one whangs through the glass in the bus door, directly on Coach's humped shadow. The bus engine revs.

It's then when one of the white men rushes up and peels Della clean away from Mr. Charles. Another man grabs Mr. Charles's jacket and runs him onto the bus so he sprawls against the big wheel. The driver hollers to get down but the whole band is at the windows anyway. They can hardly see Della in the dim yellow light of the parking lot because the men have her backed up to the bus and they are all around her. Yellow arms are moving at her. Mason goes flying out of the bus.

Coach's cussing has brought up some faces to the football bus windows. He knows his job is worth not letting any boy off the bus, and surely not a colored one. Yet somehow he can't stand to drive away and leave what is happening here. And look what that gets him: in half a minute, Attis Fuller is screaming behind him and Coach is screaming back at him, using his full weight to hold the kid off.

Mason has gone right for Della, wedging himself between her and one man, his arms out, those long skinny arms guarding her. He shrieks *Stop it Stop it Stop it*. Della slides out from behind him and crawls onto the bus. Mr. Charles pulls her up the steps and shoves her behind him. Her uniform is torn and though she is crying her face is set and hard.

Mason flails, sputtering blood. His head has been banged against the bus, his nose flaps against one cheek. When they start to kick him he falls and curls up his hands gripping his burning genitals. After a few kicks, the men begin to fade back, except for one who squats down to him and punches his mouth, snapping Mason's head back. Mason tastes metal and salt, and coughs out the bottom half of his front teeth.

This last man is uncrouching, slipping off the brass knuckles when someone barging out of the darkness slaps him across his face so hard he reels and falls into the oyster shell. This is Mr. Flynn who later will be relieved he lost his gun in the bayou because if he'd had it he cannot be one hundred percent sure he would have fired straight up at the Pleiades or Orion's sword arm. Mr. Flynn kneels down. He cannot say Vidi now because he did not see, not soon enough, not this time. Hooking an arm around Mason's chest, he hoists him halfway up so Mr. Charles can haul Mason's long body up the steps into the bus.

EVVIE DRAWS MASON'S face with the marks on it, and afterward, when they have sunk below the skin. She draws him again and again because in the shading of his eyes, in the weighted angle of his lips, the matte white of his skin, she is sure she can define this change. Mason is listless and doesn't mind. The dentist has pulled his stumps and he refuses to go to school until he gets his teeth.

One afternoon the doorbell rings; Della and her mother have come to thank Mason. They could have telephoned but only a visit suited Mrs. Jefferson's idea of correct. They decline refreshments and do not unbutton their coats, since there is only the one thing to say. "Was brave of your boy." For a second then Evvie glimpses the old Mason: his swollen face darts up, a quick light flickering his eyes. The two mothers, Mrs. Jefferson and Mrs. Budinger, their lips compressed, shake their heads and make a murmuring noise together.

Evvie draws Mason over when he gets his new front teeth, straight, a shade or two whiter than the real ones to the sides. The face emerging from the paper startles her—the even teeth, the broadened nose which puts a ruggedness into her brother's face—Mason's become handsome. Only, his nose slants a little to the left so that he doesn't seem to look head on anymore.

When he returns to class, he and Della exchanges Hi's, shyly; they don't write any more notes in Latin. In twenty-five years the ACLU will make a blind call to attorney D.K. Jefferson who will hesitate, then, in a bout of self-commun-ion, accept their case: the principle at stake applies to the rights of any group. Her client, a KKK Grand Cyclops, is ap-propriately shocked when he sees her. But fingering her di-ploma, some plaques, he grins, delighted suddenly and sly. Della reminds herself that the piercing calm which is her impetus for defending the case will come to her now and again. She block-prints the man's name and title on the first sheet of a new legal pad, sighing mentally. Her teenage son, she knows, will refuse to speak to her.

Now everyone leaves Latin class one by one. Only Mr. Flynn is the same, declining verbs as if there is always some-one in the room sweetly asleep. He sprinkles jokes and puns into the grammar. If any one of his sober class smiles, he is pleased. On the day before Christmas vacation, someone con-quers a passage and looks up—Mr. Flynn is even more pleased. He drops the fountain pen into his pocket bare nib down and stands back from the lectern folding his hands. Mason does not tap Della as he would have before so they can smile together. Della does not as Attis once burned to see glance at him with complicity brimming her eyes. Each face turns alone to the ink spot blossoming on Mr. Flynn's shirt. From the private bounds of their desks, each watches the blue assume its indelible shape.

# Move into it,
# Babies

OUR FATHER JACK had a purposeful stride and destination fixed in his eyes. He never ambled or sauntered or cut us much slack for having to take two steps to his one. Not that it escaped his attention we were children—just that to him we were Eileen and Patrick, miniature individuals. It was exhilarating to be spoken to as such. Jack respected our opinions, he trusted us to understand his, our household sang with gravity. We became serious people. To this day we exercise an uncanny ability to focus, almost an allegiance, when someone speaks to us with unguarded sincerity, from the heart, because our father spoke no other way. We are superb listeners. And now Patrick is a golf pro who spends his life playing, and I am a professional liar.

While he was black-haired and wind-burned, which is to say young and well, Jack read to us most nights from *The Book of Knowledge*, a leatherbound companion set to the encyclopedias he was proud to have bought us. I remember the exciting mix of literature and science facts, both of which I came to class as simply stories. "Dick Whittington and his

Cat," wandering the gray, bumpy streets of London; "The House of Seven Gables," which I visualized as arches, two hands touching at the fingertips; "Shiva, God of India," "How We Get Linen." I still recall the words from "The Glory of Grass"; my eager senses confused themselves and hearing the names was like tasting candies. Quaking grass, timothy, manna, reed, tufted aira. Grass stems are hollow, flowers occur in spikelets, and the blades are filled with delicate perfumes.

Then Jack got sick and our mother, Paula, desperate. We learned assorted medical terms at this time, manic depression, paranoia, schizophrenia, chemical imbalance, genetic predisposition, lithium. These tasted like ice cubes. Jack stopped working and we had to move to a rent house, a terrible blow for Paula. The bottom half of her face set differently from then on: she folded her mouth in a wounded way, while thrusting her chin forward, so that she developed, cutting downward from her lips, two sullen lines like a dummy's hinges. The rent house was large—that was important to Paula; she chose the largest one—but odd. Light switches were placed in bizarre locations, on the far sides of rooms; we felt our way through the dark to get to them. Some were above our heads, as though not meant to be handled by children. But we were big now; we adjusted ourselves to reaching. Rooms were constructed without flow, stuck together any which way. The garage opened onto the porch which opened without preamble onto the sad, matted carpet of the living room, where Jack often sat at night when the pills wore off. Until we got used to the place, Patrick and I kept bumping into each other in the dining room, a windowless oblong dead center of the house where a hall should have gone.

Paula had taken a job as night auditor at a steakhouse, tallying the receipts. She left for work at suppertime. She looked funny dressed up, in a straight gray skirt, with clip-on earrings that numbed her earlobes and her hair managed backward some way. Sometimes she forgot makeup. Rubbing her face which already looked skinned, Paula left Patrick and me with this message: we should be able to help Jack. We were 16 and 18 and her saying this made it so. We did not discuss it because Patrick and I did not discuss, period; we simply began to drift by each other in unofficial shifts—to take turns sitting with Jack. Patrick would blow in from golf; I'd vacate the couch and slide away. Later when I slipped back in, Patrick and Jack would both be staring at the television.

Jack's eyes glittered. He radiated dread, and no matter what Paula believed, the dread was real. I would have sworn Patrick felt it, too. Close to Jack, you grew afraid and ashamed. No matter that you didn't want to, or that you wanted other things, a lot of which you didn't even know what they were— you learned fear. It was a lesson conveyed by invisible rays, from his body to yours: your body absorbed and held fear. Sometimes in his frustration Jack got angry. The anger didn't clear away bad feeling but subsided back into him and so it was an ugly thing. He looked ugly then, his mouth twisted with sarcasm. I didn't know how Patrick felt about it but I felt it was unworthy of Jack, unlike how he truly was in-side—or at least, how he wanted to be.

Still we tried to talk to him. "Oh good," Jack used to say, when as toddlers we awoke from naps, stumbled sleepily to the couch beside him and flopped over again. Now he'd say, "Oh good," sometimes, perfunctorily, almost under his breath, when we came in from school, but not much after that. Once I told Jack I loved him, and a huge sigh like a festering thorn came out of him. He said he so needed to hear that.

Patrick and I bumbled, and blamed ourselves for wearing out. One time, at Paula's pleading, I stopped Jack from walk-ing around the backyard cracking a bullwhip. I was supposed to dissuade him; neighbors were watching, the new ones she avoided. I was scared to go out there. I hated Jack's ugliness, I hated Paula's begging. But I didn't go numb-eyed like Patrick; I slunk into my hard duty. This day, Jack apologized, humbly. "It's . . . satisfying," he said. I took the whip from him and struck it—it whistled and jerked my arm in the socket—and as far as I could see, Jack was right. It seemed like the whip was driving badness at least a short distance away from me. I gave it back to him, thus betraying Paula. Another night, Jack had his pocketknife out, paring his nails. He ignored or did not notice the blood running from the quick of his fingers. After he lurched off to bed, Patrick lunged around the rent-house living room with his putter, poking it into corners, passing it over Jack's chair like it was a uranium detector. Since Patrick's motive was clear to me at a glance—*Was there some deadly germ in the atmosphere surrounding Jack? Could we disperse it? Fight it? Cure it? Could we catch it?*—I asked for no explanation, he offered none. Neither of us mentioned Jack. Impassive as usual, Patrick retreated to his room; a crash from the putter and nothing more was heard from there.

As it did not seem our efforts helped either one of our parents, Patrick took to spending hours on the course where he worked, and putting till midnight in the backyard, which was helpfully dirt. He dug it full of holes. Paula, fearing the landlord, admonished him about this but I think she feared more Patrick's unnerving calm, his absolutely clear gaze like an x-ray of air. So she let him dig holes. There were some benefits to his mad dedication; he lettered that year, and though only a sophomore assumed second position on the Port Sabine team.

I had been on the track team, a brief experience. In 1969, Port Sabine wasted no track season, or pretty satin uniforms, on girls; a single, city-wide free-for-all was held. We ran in our regular shorts and Keds. I was third leg of the 200 yd relay, one of two white girls sandwiched between two black, the genuine speed, who informed us they'd beat our asses if we lost it for them. We won. Our relay team did not hug itself in congratulation. The black girls slapped each others' palms. Then Caroline, the anchor, smacked Janet's palm and Janet, second leg, catching on, turned to me and slapped mine. We all laughed, delighted with our rough, fast selves. It felt good, and it stuck, maybe, that success, because as Patrick stalked the greens, I began to run away. Surreptitiously, so as not to give any additional pain. Any errand became a ticket. When I slid behind the wheel of the Dodge, my blood rushed loose as if from a tourniquet.

Sent for prescriptions or groceries or whatever cheap, benign item I could think of to need, I looped far out by the Texaco refinery to wait for the first minute of night. As the plant lights switched on, the dreary, intestinal convolution of gray pipe and tanks and welded stacks and flares burning off methane disappeared: glimmering upward from the same foundation there appeared a flaming diamond city. I drove by the port to watch the cargo ships in the turning basin, the tugs herding them, nipping at the vast hulls loaded with rice or steel pipe or pine from the sawmills, and the port lights a gleam floating on the water. One night I put on red lipstick because it lay there on the Dodge's seat beside me escaped from Paula's purse, and found myself in the dark light of a beer bar out on Fannett. When, after a few dances, I said I wasn't supposed to be there, I was supposed to be home, the limber old cowboy twirling me under his arm murmured, "Ain't we all?"

I DID NOT plan to take Jessie Martin riding with me. We lived in her neighborhood now, in our rent house, but I did not mean to associate with her. I just walked into the 7-11,

93

scooped up Paula's loaf of Rainbo bread. It asked me to swing it by its plastic tail, so I did, and my left hand grabbed a red and white pack of Pall Malls and an irresistible magenta lighter. I was alert to color. Some nights I thought I'd pile on one of everything up by the counter—gumball, jerky, peanut patty, sunglasses, key chain, pickle. I wanted one of everything, the brighter the better. Jessie was already in line, a green bottle of Boone's Farm canted on her hip.

In elementary school, I'd thought of her as a broad, shaggy-haired shetland pony. She wore stocky saddle shoes and relished her size; she'd stomp your toes when she got mad. Once, chasing on the playground, I threw a miscalculated glance behind me to check that I'd outrun her and plowed into tree-like Raymond Doucette, biting my tongue so hard blood dripped down my chin. She didn't catch me, but she got me. You didn't get away from Jessie.

She'd grown into a Clydesdale of a girl, tall, wide-boned, thick-fleshed, with coarse hair of a mixed blonde tint—like hay, which appears in different lights yellow or greenish or tan. Her breasts lofted her loose shirt like a tent. I didn't and I never would have anything like them. She wasn't nervous about getting carded. "Eileen Powell, old wet towel," she said. She put a little irony into this tired chant, a nod to how long we'd known and endured each other. "What's going on?"

I had a repertoire of silent pejoratives to rhyme with Martin. "Nothing," I said.

A skinny guy ahead of her with leather work gloves waggling from his back pocket smirked at me. I'd seen him lean back and pretend to reach for a package of jerky strips in hopes of rubbing against Jessie's chest. Jessie had noticed, too, and simply tilted the Boone's Farm so it jabbed his spine like a gun barrel.

I didn't literally care but I asked her what she was up to tonight.

"Nothing." Jessie thumped a much-folded five on the counter and pressed the bottle between her breasts to show she was not letting go without a fight. There was a nice beat of tension as the gray-haired clerk's fingers curled in from the register. "Lemme see some ID," he said.

Jessie glowered and spilled an unimaginative story about how she'd left it at home but all the time staring at him like she could squash him, which she could. Knuckles on the counter, he lowered his eyes and let her run down. She threw a glance back at me. *Liar liar pants on fire* was the other chant historically directed at me, from the time I'd claimed my grandfather was a Choctaw Indian and described how Choctaws walked, toe first then heel. Unfortunately some of the class had tried out this method. I could think of two hardluck stories that might work for Jessie and any number better than the drivel she was giving the man but I shrugged; why should I? Finally she said, "Well . . ." she stamped the cement floor here, ". . . to you, too!" She shoved the Boone's Farm at him, and it caught an edge and circled like a dime till he grabbed its neck. Jessie knocked the door open with the flat of her hand.

When I got outside, cars were shooting by on the highway. One flicked on its lights. A flock of birds fanned over the bank clock, flowed back away from it, oozed over again, not getting anywhere. The March dusk was as neutral as a blank page. Only Jessie, leaning against the wall by the newspaper machines, reminded me the evening was actual time. "Tough luck," I said, and she glared at me like she had at the clerk.

"You used to make up shit," she accused. "Why didn't you help me?"

"It's good to think these things out in advance, Jessie," I said and to my surprise, her foot slid down from the wall and she just nodded like I was right. "Well I don't suppose you want to ride around." Jessie surprised me again.

"Get in the car," I said.

The car doors made a haunted-house creak. *Errrrk.* "Where did you get this heap?" Jessie demanded as I pushed the button for reverse. The Dodge bucked into gear.

Jack had been obliged to buy a car after he let the floor boards cave through on his old one. He was already half out of the world by then because he just wrote out a shaky check to a salesman who claimed this Dodge with its oval fins and push button transmission was a classic. "Patrick won it, hustling golf," I told her.

Jessie knew Patrick worked at the course, caddying, mowing, sweeping and locking up, so he could play for free. That's the thing about a story; some of it has to be true. "Like hell, Eileen," she said, but she wasn't sure. I kept my foot on the brake while I polished my glasses. My hair fell forward and hid my face but she probably saw me smiling into my lap. She snapped on the radio and lurched back into the wide bench seat.

As a concession, I asked her about Blane Pennick, who I heard she'd been going out with. Blane was a rich kid, goodlooking, slower-moving than a regular, jumpy high school boy. He was 6'3" and heavy as a man, the hollows of cheek, jaw, and adam's-apple already filled in. He had nowhere extra to grow; he was done. It was hard to imagine Blane with his slacks and his ironed shirts stomping around with Jessie in the places her family might go, the K-Mart, the shouting Baptist church, crabbing at dawn with one Martin kid trailing a line and another a bag of old chicken parts.

"Yep," she answered me distantly, turning her head to survey a billboard for the Shrine Circus. "Blane be the man."

White kids were talking like black ones then, trying it out. Sometimes they saved serious stuff to say in black, so that if anybody challenged them, they could pretend it was a joke. They could get down off it then. But Jessie wasn't doing that. I'd given her a chance to crow, and I wondered why she didn't.

We flew down I-10 with the windows rolled down, letting our hair beat our faces. The radio squawked raceway ads *Saturday Night! Saturday Night!* and dribbled Herman's Hermits. I couldn't get my cigarette lit with one hand in all the wind. Jessie reached over and plucked the cigarette and lighter from me, lit it in her mouth, and handed it back. She drew another from the pack for herself. "I don't have cooties," she said, "so stop thinking I do." Then she grimaced and said, "This is stupid."

And that was what I was thinking, not that she had cooties but that it was stupid to have stuck myself with Jessie Martin when, if I'd been by myself, I could have gone to one of the solitary places I liked to go. I had more than the port and Texaco twinkling at night. Twice I'd loitered on the slat wood breezeway of the Boondocks, a fishing-camp-turned-restaurant built over the bayou, tossing slim jim pieces to the alligator. Both times a bartender—the hostess sent him—came and told me if I wasn't going to take a table I should go on home. But I was not ready to go home.

I said to the thin-chested, stout-bellied bartender with the wedding ring it was my mom and dad's anniversary and they told me to get lost for an hour. His elbow elbowed my elbow vicariously; from down in his throat he said, "Hey, baby doll, don't take it personally." The time they sent out the young bartender with the springy knees, I heard myself saying the army'd called my brother's number and he had zero deferments to save him from southeast Asia. Sadly I flung a pinch of slim jim, the alligator cruised forward, and the bartender murmured, *Thank you, asthma.* Both of them let me linger until dusk, when the cypress and spikey bayonet were black and the upsurge of the alligator's eyes had just about blended with the bayou.

But now I was saddled with Jessie and when Jessie said "stupid," she meant the radio. "I can't listen to this crap," she said. "Teen Angel" was on, with the backup wooos and the megaphone voice like the singer is stranded in an empty warehouse. Jessie said, "She's dead and he's still nagging her to say she loves him. God, let the poor girl rest." She was smoking without any hands, squinting against the smoke.

I regretted now not helping her out; it would have been nice to have passed the Boone's Farm, koolaid with electricity in it. "What's your problem?" I asked her.

Jessie wrenched the radio dial over to KJET, the black station, asking me had I ever been by there and then smiling as a pearly night voice invited us to stay with him, babies, because he would be here tonight all night until the stroke of midnight, filling our ears with magic.

"Barry Van Horn, six to twelve," Jessie said. She twisted the volume and Bobby Hebb's sexy whisper surged out and then Joe Tex and Archie Bell & the Drells and the choreographed energy of the Temptations, and we drove, and everything began to feel a little less stupid. The next surprise of the evening was that Jessie could sing. On the higher notes, the roughness peeled away from her voice like moss off a clean branch. She held the note cleanly, without warbling. I sang a chorus with her, and it was almost like we were going somewhere.

Jessie quoted, "'You made life so rich, You know you could a been some money.' Now that's lyrics." I'd turned off onto a side road and we were driving forty, kicking up a white dust behind us. Jessie said she had to go so when I saw a place, I pulled over and cut the engine. The Dodge shook and died but she made no move to get out. That was when a further cue or a clue sounded in my mind and I knew to suspect her motivation. But I had read a lot of books—lengthy ones like

*Moby Dick, Valley of the Dolls, Crime and Punishment, Fanny Hill*, whole volumes of *The Book of Knowledge*—and they had made me patient. You will find out if you wait. I set aside my curiosity to watch the evening.

Beyond a weedy ditch, cypress trees were knobby-kneed in the standing water, their tops budding in the tall air. If it had still been light enough we could have seen their color, rusty-red like the methane flares—leaves on fire. We sat there, the car doors wide, with our orange-tipped cigarettes. The fuse in the car light was burned out and the soft dark settled on us, peaceful after we'd been driving so fast. In summer we'd have had bug problems but as it was, in spring, we only had bug singing and frog singing, prolonged and serene and lulling. They held the continuous note—or new ones joined in as others dropped out to breathe and that's how they worked their seamless chorus, singing and breathing and singing and breathing. Or maybe that's how they breathed, by singing.

"God, it's quiet out here," Jessie complained.

I leaned back on the seat, letting my hair hang over. "I think it's loud," I said.

"Insects are loud? Jeez, you must live in a graveyard."

I said I did not live in a graveyard.

She knocked my knee. "No offense, Eileen Powell."

Jessie said she'd met Janis Joplin's little sister at a party and she looked just like anybody else. It was a disappointment.

"What did you expect her to look like?"

"Janis. Beads and bellbottoms. Maybe a tattoo. You know in high school, they treated Janis like shit? My cousin went to school over there and he said they laughed at her, said she smelled funny. Now look." Jessie's voice hardened with gleeful scorn. "She can eat them alive." Turning her face away, she admitted—and admission was an uncharacteristic mode for Jessie—one of her daydreams was to be like Janis. Holding down her own band. A roadie with a powderpuff to mop her face when she stepped offstage. She could live that life.

"Not me," I said. I wanted to live my moment but not in the glory spot, carrying it all. I'd rather have been backup, the one far back in the dark, letting my voice loose in the swell before the last drum crash.

Jessie said I lacked ambition.

So we sat there like in school, where we never had a word to say to each other. The bayou breathed around us. The cypress were the father trees and the clubby knees their huddled children listening to stories, and the whole family rose from the flat sheen of water like they grew through a mirror.

Jessie extracted another cigarette from the pack and commented on the house we'd moved into. Having grown up in the neighborhood, she knew the house's history. A family named Fertitta had owned it. Every time Mrs. Fertitta had another baby, old man Fertitta would have some lumber delivered and start hammering away on another room.

"That explains it," I muttered. The rent house had grown like a weed does, like a blade of wild grass, poking up wherever and however it can.

Jessie skipped on to Patrick's sideburns, which he'd let grow long. I thought the sideburns, combined with his customary lack of expression, gave Patrick a nineteenth-century, daguerreotype air; he leaned on his putter like a gentleman on an ebony cane. Jessie let this pass without comment but asked about his hustling golf. I'd got this idea from hearing the tail end of Paula's nervous ". . . not gambling, are you?" and Patrick's lame denial. I explained he just duffed around for a few shots and then once the money was out, his game radically improved. He hit a wild one occasionally to maintain the fiction, but slowly dollars came to live in

Patrick's pocket. "Wow," she said.

Jessie and I were conversing. It felt strange—as though Dick Whittington's familiar old cat had opened its mouth and talked to me.

"I heard your daddy's sick," she said then. "He's off work for a while." Since all our parents had been raggedy-head 30's kids with one pair of underwear, not working was alarming news. I noted, though, the charity of "a while," that also was uncharacteristic of Jessie; it threw me. I didn't know if my father could ever go back.

"What's wrong with him?" Jessie asked, and I knew she would have heard that, too. Everybody's fathers worked the refineries, and besides, there was that day with the bullwhip.

"He's got a malignant brain tumor that's displaced 40% of his cerebral cortex. It's created a bulge in his skull," I said.

Her nose wrinkled.

"He's got purpura," I chose a word she wouldn't know, "his blood has clotted inside his veins. If he cuts himself now, flakes sift out."

"Eileen." She flicked ash out the window, looking at me.

"His heart beats too slowly, like church bells, so he doesn't get enough oxygen. Sometimes his lips turn steel blue."

My own lips trembled. I despised what I'd said, making cheap fun of Jack. I was used to feeling superior to Jessie, as a means of self-defense. Now I did not and, defenseless, I'd turned mean, which disheartened me. "Look, Jessie," I scraped the air, trying to erase the whole subject, "it's just details. Remember that next time. You left your ID at home, Jesus."

Even that failed to incite her. This was an uncommon night. "No, really," she said.

Really those were the diseases Paula wished Jack had, symptoms the neighbors and his bosses and she could credit and pity.

Before I told Jessie what was wrong with my father, I wanted to get one thing straight so if she used this information against me, she would have to acknowledge and suffer her own spite. "You never liked me, did you?"

Smoke blew from her nose in two streams. "No," she said. "I never liked you either."

I may have seen Jessie's hand twitch or maybe I just thought it should have. Instinctively both of us knew we could no longer follow the old, playground pattern, insults, a kick or a slap. We were past that. The husky dignity of the truth separated us like a referee. So we eyed each other in the near-dark, our faces shades of gray and black and our foreheads a dull ivory white, like woodcut pictures of George Washington and Thomas Jefferson in history books.

Until finally the solemnity grew bigger than we were, and we started laughing. We laughed until we bent over and we kept on until the wildlife singing around us was startled into silence by our rude, unnatural noise.

Jessie wiped her eyes with her shirt, exposing her cotton fortress of a bra overspilled by breast. With a pang of envy, I hunted around under the seat to locate a scuffed paper napkin from the Dairy Queen to blow my nose on. I stalled. Should I tell her that on one of my sidetrips I'd visited Sister Rosa the fortune teller for a diagnosis? Maybe. After all, it was true. Better than repeating what Paula had said, bitterly and loud enough for Jack to hear, that there was not a goddamn thing wrong with him that a stiff backbone couldn't fix, that he should just haul his carcass out of that chair and go back to work. If he didn't pull himself together soon, no one would hire him back. Her night-auditor job was not cutting it and we would have to live in this shithouse forever and have only red beans and cornbread and gritty collards to eat, just like when she was a girl.

But if you use only the flat truth a story comes out too

flatly, like you are sorry for yourself. So I told Jessie I'd con-
sulted Sister Rosa and she had said—

"Wait, wait," Jessie said, "you went to see that witch?
With the sign? You, old Eileen Powell, that used to drag that
leather book around at recess because you were scared to
play baseball?"

I touched my glasses; I never could see a softball coming.
One broke my glasses once and comforting me, Jack brushed
my sweaty hair back and assured me that, besides children,
what was most worthwhile in life you couldn't see anyway.
He knelt so I could look into the pain in his face. Jack did
not scissor his meaning for any father-to-child perspective,
he talked, like always, arrow-straight, person-to-person. He
said I was like him. What would nourish my particular heart
would not be a brick house or a Cadillac car but a faith in my
own doings. In me, Eileen Powell. That, you could not buy
and without it, you might as well be dead. Gripping my arms,
he said I better know now I was going to need what I couldn't
see. Paula, fiddling with my broken frames, cut him short
with, "Oh Jack, a baseball in the head?"

"Fortunes, $5," I confirmed Sister Rosa's sign; Jessie's eyes
widened. I described Sister Rosa's snaky hair and bangel bracelets, her chihuahua, an iron pot steaming on the stove, the
pay phone in the living room, the shrine by her reading table.
Inevitably I added a vase of sandalwood incense wands, a
squat jade Buddha, and—I pedaled my arms to show Jessie—
a brass statue of Shiva the destroyer, the dancing Indian god
with the six arms and a perfectly balanced right leg, cocked
at the knee, tiny heel planted. I nudged Jessie, posing my
heel in the car. A lie but a quiet and logical one. I thought
you'd want all the gods around you when you did this kind
of work.

But the pay phone was a practical convenience for her
customers and Sister Rosa's altar was a homey production,

really—a school picture of a dark-haired girl from another time, framed by pigeon feathers her kids probably found, a loop of Christmas lights over a chipped nativity worshipped by camels and sheep and nodding shepherds, a grocery store novena candle. When Sister Rosa lit it with a kitchen match, the madonna on the glass bloomed out in shy pastels. Neither did I mention to Jessie that Sister Rosa's round face was as friendly as the moon and in her house I felt good. In my own house, my father suffered from an illness we could not see, and my mother railed against that property of the disease. But Sister Rosa's house was built on what can't be seen. Her candles and her Christmas lights, the pot of pinto beans simmering on her stove—she earned those by tinkering with the invisible. So I was ready to believe without believing, to appreciate without judging, to take anything of value, to leave what I could not use. Whatever happened there would be all right.

"So what did she say?" Jessie asked.

What did she say? Sister Rosa flipped over the queen of spades and the six of diamonds and predicted I would marry a man in uniform and live neither in Texas nor Louisiana. Then she offered to answer one question, and after hearing it, she envisioned the number 3, three weeks or months, maybe even three more years before my father might recover. For fif-, no, forty dollars she could perform a curing ritual but—having swiftly taken in my empty hands prostrate on her table—she did not push the sale. We prayed. We prayed long and hard, to Jesus and to the madonna and for all I knew to the donkey and the sheeps. Sister Rosa's bracelets rattled with the force that flowed into her wrists.

I did not tell Jessie that. I did not want to reveal that picture of me, my hands clinging together like two survivors dredged up on a riverbank. So I made up a variation. Sister Rosa, I told Jessie, had said this: my father had quenched his heart-soul. I would rather have invented a word but I did not have time to sift about for a sound that suited me.

"His what?"

Heart-soul, I repeated. It was a common occurrence. It happened sometimes since we carried a number of souls but the one my father had lost, this was the crucial one. The one God loves and takes back when we die. I showed Jessie the whole scene as I imagined it: Sister Rosa exclaimed, "See this?" She tapped the novena candle. "It's not this." She grasped the bright glass, hiding the virgin's downcast eyes. "Mira, baby, it's this.'" She pointed inside to the flickering flame. That, I explained, was Sister Rosa's analogy for the heart-soul—it was the best I could do on the spot—this flame inside the body of the glass.

Jessie sat stock still during my recital. "I'd ask you what you do to fix something like your daddy's got, but I guess the answer is you don't know."

"That's the answer," I said.

A solid, dark attention radiated from Jessie's side of the car. "Could he die?"

"No. But sometimes my mother wishes he would. And you get infected by your mother's wishing." The bug and frog song raised and thickened. I wanted to cover my ears but sound waves penetrate flesh and blood; you cannot keep them out.

Jessie said, "Hell." We sat there.

After a while, she jumped out, wiggled down her cutoffs and pissed by the ditch. She didn't even look to see if any cars were coming, which they weren't. She just squatted, keeping her legs wide so it wouldn't run onto her feet. She cupped her face in her hands, taking her time.

"Okay here's the deal," Jessie said when she got back in, being one of those people who thought when they squatted. "Will you move this damn seat back?" I did, and she spread out and let me in on the Blane Pennick problem. She told me how she'd really liked him. Not only because he was rich and popular, though that did appeal, that was almost too good to be true. If she caught herself imagining a two-story house with a breezeway and azalea bushes in the yard she stifled that, though at the edge of her vision, it dazzled her anyway. But she'd liked Blane, too, because he was as big and solid as she was. She felt good with him, like they matched in that way; what's more, he seemed to feel that same thing. She thought. Then last Friday they'd been out and run into his older sister Alison down on Liberty Street. She had scanned Jessie with a know-all gleam like Jessie was something funny. A snort of air erupted from Alison's bitty nose, like a laugh had started on its own before she could catch it. Like she couldn't help it.

"What did Blane do?"

Jessie stuck her feet up on the dashboard and crossed her arms, lifting her breasts resentfully. "Blane looked embarrassed. But not for me. Of me. Eileen, he made me feel a inch tall. Like one of those Irish fairies."

"Leprechauns?"

"Yeah, except not cute or lucky or anything. Very not cute or lucky."

Now I understood why we were sitting here on a back road by a family of bending cypress. Eileen Powell, old wet towel, was here to help her work out revenge. Everybody knew Jessie's sister Tinker had caught her husband with a woman under her new taffeta bedspread. She had not let that naked woman dress but dragged her by the hair and booted her into the yard, pelting her clothes after her. I wished I could have seen it. I enjoyed that kind of scene, as long as it wasn't happening to me. I wouldn't have gossiped about it later, either, but cherished it to me, saved it up, like money to spend on a future day.

What had Jessie done to Blane so far, I wanted to know. "Nothing. We have a date this Friday."

"Doesn't sound like you."

Well, she'd had to think about it, she said, she'd had to come to terms. But Jessie didn't pretend she hadn't seen him be ashamed of her, no use in that. Because there it was. She was a realist, she said, with a quick gloating glance, a payback for "purpura" and "daguerreotype" and maybe for "analogy."

She hesitated. Did I know Blane Pennick hadn't done it yet? The pause was Jessie's version of delicacy, a decision to ignore that I had not done it either, which we both knew she would rightly assume, tacitly agreeing, however, to shelve my virginity as a non-issue, and focus on the central problem.

I got a Pall Mall and sat back, my elbow out the window. "Go on," I said.

Jessie smiled and started in with "Midnight Hour." That's when her love would come tumbling down. She would take that boy and hold him she would do all the things she told him in the midnight hour. Up to a certain point.

"Do you get it yet?"

Why ruin the suspense? I let her tell me. Blane would be up down and all around and then she would let him have it—only the "it" would not be what he expected. Here she stopped, anticipating difficulties. Nice was too ingrained in him for him to slug her and anyway she was strong enough to handle his action. Pride glinted in her face as she made this claim. I felt it then, how she really did love herself for being big, for the sheer amount of space she owned in the world. So . . . Jessie went on, at that hot point, maybe when he stopped to tear open the rubber she knew he was carrying . . . she would sit back and tell him he slobbered when he kissed and his dick looked like a thumb, that—

I was with this story, I was having fun, I leaned over to study the justice in her eyes.

She stopped, irritated by my looking at her. "What?" she demanded.

I shook my head. "He's just gonna badmouth you," I said.

Jessie heaved herself out of the car, stomped over to the road and scooped up shells and rocks, pelted the water beneath the cypress trees. "I know he will," she called.

I followed her out. I was going to for-instance her with one of the ID excuses I'd thought up in the 7-11, as an example of cash-register-ringer vs. forget-it stories. But I went closer to home. You always have to in the end. "It would have been better if Tinker had just thrown out that woman's car keys," I told Jessie, "and kept her clothes."

Her head whipped around. Hadn't she realized how fast and how broadly the Tinker story had spread? Everybody liked it, not just me. Jessie didn't say anything, though.

She was waiting for me to.

I enjoyed that. I took off my glasses and sat down on the dewy grass, crushing a thousand hollow stems and spikelet flowers, releasing their delicate perfumes. A crescent strip, a thin, curved palm of light, held up the dark ball of the moon and it was like that palm was mine.

I smoked and watched the moon and conceived a vengeance. It was not original in any way or complicated—did not require costumes, props, extra personnel, or an exotic locale. It was simple and organic. I tossed the cigarette butt and looked away from Jessie, toward the Dodge. "If it's true like books say that you always remember your first time . . ." I had to cede a bit of power here but not too much and circumspectly I would not ask her for a confirmation. "Maybe you should do it with him."

Jessie thought I was disrespecting her. She shot me a faithless look and chunked her last shell in the water, hard.

"This is just an idea. You can take it or leave it."

She shoved her hands into her pockets. Her head was

tilted away from me. But she waited, so I went on.

"Okay. Then when he takes you home, tell him—like it's really just hit you—what you saw in the street that night. Tell him how bad he made you feel. Now after what you've just done, couldn't help doing with him, you realize you can't be with him anymore. You want a boy who's proud of you. Give him a smile, a little sad but happy too because you can go on being happy without him. You'll find that other boy someday. 'So . . .'" sincerity softened my voice, "'. . . good luck to you Blane, no hard feelings.' Lean over and give him the world's sweetest goodbye kiss, just like a sister but not quite, and look him in the eye. Go right in and shoot the bolt."

"But—"

"Then, Jessie," I overrode her, "he might badmouth you to other people but he just might not be able to badmouth you to himself, in the locked-up deep of his heart. And you'll be his first. He might not want to but he will have to remember Jessie Martin forever."

She sat down and hugged her legs to her, setting her chin on her knees. Something stirred the water, tadpoles maybe. Gentle circles broke against the cypress knobs. Finally she angled her head my way and said, "That's ambition."

I didn't know if she would do it, I knew I wouldn't ask. Jessie turned her chin back to the cypresses. I slipped my glasses back on. Venus hung beneath the new moon like a locket on an unseen chain.

WE CLIMBED IN the car again and tuned in to Question Mark & The Mysterians with "Ninety-Six Tears," theme song of grief and manipulation. Jessie slammed her door. We had a whole new mood, and she wanted to run it. "Lemme show you something, Eileen. Drive where I tell you."

So I drove as she directed, back up that road and down another one, a straightaway and then a right turn and another right. "There's nothing out here," I said. Just a maze of pine tangled in with oak, still scratchy and bare, a clump of pampas grass and swaying cattails, gray in the headlights. Finally she had me take another right, and my eyes blinked on a ball of white light like a star burning above the treetops.

The star winked out and then on again. It topped a thin wire derrick I recognized as a transmitter tower, which rose beside a low building with an expanse of lighted plate glass. As we pulled closer, into the circle of a clearing, I saw, lit up in the control booth, a handsome brown man with a mustache and a silver microphone.

"That's gotta be Barry Van Horn," Jessie whispered in a starstruck tone. One hand rested on the base of her neck. "Look at him sitting there. Doesn't he look like a present for somebody? Wave at him. Let's get him to say something to us on the radio."

But my breath had caught. How could you expect this? How could you plan for it? You could not plan for it anymore than you could plan to know what you didn't ten minutes ago—that during a numbing jaycee meeting fifteen or twenty years from now, bald Blane Pennick will bang his gavel for order, and young Jessie Martin will reverberate along the nerve endings of his skin and incite a wistful fibrillation in his flesh.

Here in all these miles of dark—this clearing and this light on, eerie and beautiful. The source, the planted foot of the rainbow, a man behind a bright window sending out music. I thought I had invented him, and now here he was, better than I had invented and provided for me to see. My stomach fluttered. Inventing him, I'd found what I really believed—that my father had wandered into himself and tripped the light off behind him and now he could not find his way out.

Because to me the man in the booth was the living picture of what my father had lost. He was the flickering inside Sister Rosa's candleglass, he was the heart-soul out there. I must have had an awful expression on my face.

Jessie inferred a different interpretation. She got up on the same high horse she was riding when she could imagine herself as the mighty Janis Joplin, and she condescended to me. "Listen, Eileen," she said. "When you're a celebrity, you're not any color at all. You're just a big old glow." She got excited. "Get closer!"

Jack's fear shivered my veins. "I'll have to go up the drive, should I go up the drive?"

Jessie pushed my shoulder. "Go up the drive, girl!"

I crept closer, braking ten feet away from the window so Jessie could wave. When the dj waved back, she squealed. She kept saying, "That's Barry Van Horn. That's him, right there."

Barry Van Horn grinned at us, bouncing in our seats. He raised his hand and blew us a kiss.

Jessie grabbed out the window, caught it, and applied it to her mouth. He blew another and she hogged that, too. It was pathetic to wrestle her for the kiss, not because it was only a puff of air, no, even today I count that kiss as worthy—generous, playful, cinnamon and sex cupped in her hands—but because just who did I imagine would win? Nevertheless, abandoning my dear self-image and any good sense, I wrestled her. I fought her for that kiss—that spark straight from the center of things. I did not want to be, like Jack, shut out. We struggled and shoved, me prying at her big fist until Jessie said, "Oh, here," and her palm popped me on the mouth with it. I tasted salt where she'd nicked my lip but I didn't care.

His fans had driven out here to nowhere and found him, and Barry Van Horn was laughing.

Accusing me of embarrassing her, Jessie ordered me to floor it. About a minute later, Sam Cook's sweet tones melted away and another issued from the dash—a clipped mellow voice that could have been riding the kilowatts from any far important place—from Chicago or New York City. Barry Van Horn said, "That one's dedicated to all you blue-eyed soul sisters out there, hiding what the good Lord gave you. Move into it, babies."

We screamed. I zigged onto the shoulder and had to zag back. Jessie collapsed on the seat, fanning her neck and between her legs, and we were buoyed up and giggling until we hit Fannett Street's flat stretch of bars and churches and the closed stores and empty streets downtown. Then Jessie folded, laying her head half-out the rolled-down window. She shut her eyes like she was sleepy and hummed. We skirted the port and soared across the overpass by the creosote plant, a dark yard stacked with treated telephone poles. A spot of wet seeped into the depression of Jessie's eye socket and stayed there, like cypress water, standing in her eye. As the creosote fumes swirled in she clamped her nose, but me, really, I never minded that dizzy smell.


I COULD SAY it was the same night I went driving with Jessie that I ran into Patrick in the rent-house kitchen, though that strikes me as too neat. Truth is, neat or not, it could have been that same night because I believe I was swinging a loaf of bread. I came in through the garage to the porch, heard the television bawling and knew Jack was awake. He was bent over in his chair, elbows on his knees, his forehead laid heavy in his hands. He made me feel so helpless I stalked right past him. He jerked up, disoriented, but after a second he knew me and murmured from old habit "Oh good." I turned. Then he saw himself as he was in front of his child and was ashamed. His face sagged into the ugly slackness. I wanted to punish him for casting us all into his dark. But I also wanted to sink my fingers in his face and rearrange it. I wanted to reach into his chest and into his brain and gather everything in there, to splice cells with arteries with dangling synapses until they all lit up. I wanted to be like Jack because he warned me I would need what I couldn't see and he was right and that was like blessing who I was. I wanted to be like him because I loved him. I didn't want to be anything like him. I wanted him to read me a story.

I walked across the dark kitchen and rested my hand on the wall by the light switch, inches above my head. Finally I flipped it on. I turned and pitched the bread toward the dinette, then flinched; there was Patrick. He'd been sitting there all the time, on the counter drinking a coke.

"Hey," he said, in a low voice.

Later it dawned on me that he was actually waiting for me to come home. Because you'd want to tell about an event like this. Paula wouldn't be home till one and Jack was Jack—he would have labored so valiantly to appreciate it that by the time the smile surfaced on his lips you'd have been on your knees. So there was only me.

Patrick told me that that evening, after the course closed, he'd shot a hole in one. He got down from the counter and acted it out for me. He hunched over an imaginary club, fitted and resettled his hands, positioned his knees, dug in. Then he rared back, swung, and blasted the ball. Shading his eyes, he charted the white spot as it rose, arced, flew and flew and flew, hit, and ran straight into the hole. Patrick showed me his double take, how he'd thrown the club. Though miniaturized, these gestures were more animated than any I'd seen from him. I understood two things: that like mine Patrick's life was surging on in a secret way that could not be stopped, and that his reenaction was only a mild facsimile. When he mimed a leap into the air, he made me see the original—wild, heedless, triumphant. He landed in a crouch so as not to thump the linoleum and shudder Jack in the next room. I still hadn't said anything, but I think my mouth was ajar.

Patrick mumbled that the hole-in-one was unofficial—course was closed, nobody saw. He wasn't smiling, exactly. The only way I could tell he was happy was by the occupied look in his eyes. I went to work to name it. Patrick was bemused, intoxicated maybe, by this rare accomplishment, yes, but also by himself so present inside it. I realized he was waiting for me to say something.

I lifted my hand and glared until he lifted his. I slapped it. "Way to go," I whispered to my brother. Breaking into a grin, Patrick put his hand back up again. We slid our palms together.

# Terrell's House

JAKE is on the other side of the big glass doors to St. Mary's emergency room, hands jammed in his armpits, on the lookout for her. The backwards A's cap mashes his shoulder-length hair out of his face; his furrowed expression makes Margaret run the last few steps. She starts to ask what exactly the situation is but her son doesn't give her the chance. "They already took him back there," Jake blurts. "He made me bring him a suitcase with his stuff and he made me wait while he put on a clean shirt. He threw up. Mom. I had to button it for him."

"He was talking? He could talk?"

"Yeah, he can talk. It's—" Jake steers her away from the reception desk, toward the treatment area. A guard presses a button and the heavy automatic doors swing open; people in white and hospital green stride in and out of the rooms. Craning, Margaret sees blue curtains and feet splayed out, tennis shoes, boots. Not Terrell's.

"Mom, it's here," Jake finishes, meaning his grandfather's pain is where he indicates; he runs his fingers in a straight line from collarbone to mid-chest. Margaret just looks at him.

Her father has been having TIA's, little strokes which incapatitate him briefly. Fearing the big one, Margaret expects to find him blank-faced and silent at the least, at the worst unconscious, left or right side drooping, snoring the horrible snore of the brain-damaged.

But Terrell is cordoned off behind a curtain on an ER gurney, shiny wingtips crossed, bitching at a nurse trying to draw blood. His shirt is fresh but he hasn't shaved; his chin is furred with white whiskers Margaret hardly ever sees. Jake slides bedside—or gurney-side—and leans on the wall.

"Please, sir, let me do my job." The nurse bows her head further over Terrell's arm.

"You're not a nurse." Terrell's chin is out. "You're a goddamn out-of-work riveter."

The nurse's jaw edges sideways. "I'm telling you, sir, I do not have to tolerate obscenities." She sticks Terrell again; not a drop of blood appears in her tube. She calls for backup. Another nurse sticks him. No blood. They call a third nurse, who brings a new needle and tries again.

"What do you imposters really do for a living?" Terrell growls.

Margaret is trying to follow a monitor above and behind Terrell's head. She is not understanding this situation, cannot seem to grasp what kind of stroke this is. The numbers fly everywhere. 200. 37. 0. If the S means systolic and the D is for diastolic, at this moment Terrell has no blood pressure. But he is sitting up on the gurney, fierce-faced, brewing insults.

"Later," a nurse brushes off Margaret when she presses for an explanation.

Jake peers at the thermometer device, a tiny screen; confusion sweeps his face. Margaret checks its report: 93. What? The fierceness leaves Terrell as he turns to Jake and Margaret, who takes hold of his arm to comfort him. His arm is freezing. Nurses are still bent over his other arm, switching needles. Periodically Terrell flinches, cursing at another needle-stick. A technician, a heavy black woman with white shot through her hair, has wheeled in an EKG machine, hooked him to that.

"I'm griping," Terrell warns the technician. "I'll bite your head off." Margaret knows it's the grizzled streaks in this woman's hair, that she is still working, on her feet, at an age not so much less than Terrell's, that have curbed his temper.

The technician responds in kind. "Oh, I done heard that, sir." She smiles. "I surely did."

He softens at the older woman's coy smile; any offering of kindness disarms Terrell. When she was a teenager Margaret used this; later on she hurt for Terrell, that a feather of kindness could blow him over.

"I'm gonna—" Terrell's cheeks puff. A nurse points to a nearby cabinet. Jake jumps over and rifles through it, tossing aside boxes of gauze to grab a stack of bedpans. He thrusts two or three, still stacked, into his grandfather's hands. Terrell vomits into them.

A bearded doctor in Birkenstocks and socks, with a clipboard and a pleasant expression, asks Terrell, "Have you ever had a heart attack before?"

Terrell lifts his head slowly, accepts the Kleenex from Margaret, grinds out deliberately, "Before when?"

"O-kay." Breezy, the doctor checkmarks the clipboard. "Cardiologist will be right in."

Terrell blinks at Margaret, turns his head away and stares out into the room. His mouth sets. Behind the curtains are other sick or hurt people, but Terrell's gaze is inward. Margaret's worried eyes consult with Jake's.

The cardiologist glances at the scraggy lines on the technician's readout, slides between Jake and Margaret for a look at Terrell. He does not touch him. Instead he angles to smile ruefully at Margaret. Slides away.

Margaret runs her fingers through her hair. All right, she may be way behind here, but she has got this much: This is no TIA. Terrell is having a heart attack. The monitors behind Terrell's head allow her to see inside his misfunctioning body, to see the blood stopped, the heart misfiring, choking, rhythmless. It is all happening behind his back. Margaret herself is operating in two opposing modes: as soon as one part of her totes up the inexorable signs, another part rejects them, countering: But this is your father. This is Terrell. She fails to snag the speedy cardiologist; the hall is vacant. She returns to her father's side. Terrell clutches the bedpans, vomiting again. This time she doesn't put the Kleenex in his hand. During some interim she did not know was occurring, a line was crossed. She wipes his mouth herself and he lets her.

Jake, his face flickering as he tries not to register anything, offers to go call Uncle Bill.

"That's a good idea." Margaret searches her wallet for her phone card. She should have thought of calling her older brother herself. He's in Seattle but he ought to know about the problem here.

"Old Bill," Terrell says, "Bill the Pill." He lies back, has to catch his breath. "Jakey," he says, snaring Jake's hand, and Jake, sidestepping out from behind the gurney, Jake who has shied from all embrace the last few years, stops and lets his hand be held. Terrell's watery glance rolls over his grandson. "This is a fine man, isn't it, Margaret?" It's a thing Terrell does, a Terrell-trick to cut emotion, speaking in third person though Jake is right there.

"He sure is," Margaret answers.

Terrell is quiet for a while, contemplating, his gaze far away. Though a droplet of blood streaks the inside of his elbow, he has stopped protesting the nurses, still working with vials and needles.

Then he asks, "Is today the 19th?" Jake is nodding, helpful, but Terrell doesn't see that; his long habit of communication is with Margaret. "The 19th, Mae Mae?"

"Yes, but don't be worrying now about anything you had to do."

"The 19th of April." Terrell pronounces the date to himself, as though tasting it. "April 19th, 1994. 1994," he echoes.

Then—a lurch beneath her breastbone—Margaret knows why he's asked. He's thinking this could be the date that closes his parentheses. But she doesn't believe in that.

His head tilts toward them again, though he doesn't look into their faces. "And Mae Mae," he goes on shakily, distantly, "she is a pretty smart girl. She is a fine girl." He fumbles some of their fingers in his hand, his grip loose and cool, and then he lets them go.

A woman in a business suit with a clipboard mashed to her chest calls for a member of Terrell's family. Of course, there will be papers to sign. Margaret starts forward and then stops; it doesn't seem right to leave Terrell now.

"You go right on, Mae Mae. Go on." Terrell pats the air where her hand was, his thick eyebrows drawn together as though he is listening. Fuzzy caterpillers, Jake used to call them, and Terrell would oblige by hopping them around on his forehead.

"Dad, I—"

"ICU," a nurse says, pushing them back. "Third floor." Two nurses, collecting the IV stand, roll Terrell off to a far elevator while Margaret and Jake trail along. "Hey wait," Jake barks, lopes back toward the treatment room.

A third nurse, a tall woman with plain brown hair and a pen poised over her clipboard—everyone has a clipboard—asks Margaret about heroic measures, in the event her father—the nurse's voice joggles exactly like a skip in a record—in the event her father . . . "doesn't do well."

"Doesn't do well? No machines if it's no use, if that's what you mean. Look, is that what you—" The nurse's eyes dart away to a clock on the wall; she jots, she x's, she's gone.

Margaret is squinting after her when Jakes dashes out of the ER room again and gallops up to the gurney. The two nurses shake their heads. "No, please take it," Jake says with the reasonableness Margaret finds so mysterious; where did he get it? "He'll want his stuff." The nurses exchange a glance. They pile Terrell's suitcase onto the gurney, the shaving kit, the good pajamas.

Jake holds up his hand as the elevator doors clank shut.

119

ON A MORNING last month, sitting with his daughter in the backyard swing, Terrell asked her to tell him where he went during these awful spells, these TIA's.

"You go still, Dad," Margaret said. "Your eyes glaze over and you don't blink when we wave our hands in front of your face. You don't answer us."

"It's so odd not to know," Terrell murmured. "You live in this body all your life and then it goes crazy on you." Terrell patted his legs, his belly under the pressed sport shirt, held out his arms.

"My turf," he said. "My temple."

Just when Margaret thought he'd roar and spit about the course of things, Terrell turned tender. Rubbed a hand over the smooth chin, redolent with Aqua Velva. Nodded. "You've done good, old son," he praised his body. "Did everything a man was promised."

Jake came toward them with coffee cups on a tray. Margaret had ordered her son to do this, though the instant coffee would be haphazardly stirred and he would have oversugared the black stuff and forgotten cream. She studied him, large-framed and skinny, as he bent his knees, kept even so as not to spill anything. He'd remembered to wear the newer jeans in deference to Terrell, who frowns at the holey ones which showcase Jake's hairy legs and huge boxer shorts through the rips. To Terrell's mind, dressing like that is foolish when you own a decent pair of pants, and disrespectful to those who don't.

"Thank you, son." Terrell took his cup. Margaret took hers, preparing herself in advance not to grimace at the taste. Jake draped himself bonelessly on the plastic-strip chaise lounge to drink his. He didn't drink much of it, would have preferred a Snapple.

They sipped, together, as if it were the way it used to be, the three of them at the supper table, in the years Margaret went back to school and they moved in with Terrell—in the days Terrell stood in for Jake's absent father, natty umpire of

120

little league games, a red plaid bow tie at his neck beneath the chest protector. Terrell had read Margaret stories pronouncing with excruciating accuracy every "the" and "a." By the time he got to Jake, though, his pleasure was memory. Hat tipped back, elbows on his knees, he offered up passionate testimonials to the hardships of the Depression or the trials of the common man.

Jake, about eight, covers fixed, listening. Terrell on a kitchen chair by the bed.

". . . and he said she couldn't vote, this little gray-haired colored woman—" Margaret knew that story. She'd been there, a scared child of seven, clutching Terrell's khakis. Back in Port Sabine in a school gym. Terrell, second in line and rigid as a bird dog, listening in on the scene in front of him. Finally leaning around the woman, threatening *Goddamn you, Mister, let her vote*, popping a rolled newspaper against the table.

". . . and how it used to be, Jakey, on the crews, nobody but a white man could rise above the grade of laborer. Not even to foreman. Company spelled it out. Imagine now," Terrell would say, his face thoughtful. "Imagine that your life. No matter how hard you worked, you could never be anything but a low grade laborer. How would you like it?" Jake's eyes narrowing. Terrell rubbing his palms together. "I would a lived my life in a rage."

Jake, at twelve, the budding defender, shifting to the shut down of a timber business, saying softly, "Look, Terrell, we have to save the earth." Not yet old enough to humor Terrell but since Terrell's issues were solved in Jake's mind—he didn't want to hate anyone for their color or deny them votes or jobs—to him these issues were history, already solved in the world at large. He had a friend, Jamal, he didn't see what the big deal was. Jake staked out a new battlefield.

"Doubtless, we have to save the earth," Terrell agreed, though he would not have agreed with another soul who tendered that opinion. "Oh they are. . . the worst!" he'd cry of environmentalists, claiming their willingness to sacrifice others sprang from the most innocent and smallest of hearts. So, after agreeing, his voice trembling with intensity, Terrell would launch his rebuttal: "Oh but Jakey. Tell that to a saw-mill worker who can't feed his babies. Tell that to him after you've cut out his backbone, taken his pride. Do you think what holds us up is puny old bone and muscle?"

"Without the earth there won't be any backbones," Jake said. "No babies, either. We'll all die off," he went on mildly, "one by one. Imagine how sad that would be for everybody, Terrell." And Terrell, enchanted and mystified as was Margaret herself by this new territory in his grandson, a softness that would not be moved, would almost let the argument go.

Not always fine, though, not always agreeable.

Terrell cornering Jake on the couch after Jake's father came back and asked to see him. Gave Margaret a big shock on the phone. Jake about fourteen, already holey, rattling around loose in his big clothes, hair shooting in and out of his face.

"You wanna see him?" Terrell, trying hard to be judicious, chin out. They'd had a ballgame planned, the local minor league team, Terrell buoyed, had his good hat on, a wind-breaker, then this phone call.

Jake tipped his head sideways, raising his eyebrows which were thick like Terrell's, a little head-tip that could have meant anything. What it meant, Margaret knew, was Yes, I don't want to hurt your feelings but Yes.

"You should go then. We can see a ballgame anytime. Any old day."

Jake, inched forward, quiet. Terrell, patting his pockets, collecting his keys, a dusty pack of cigars Margaret thought he'd forgotten about, raising one hand. "I'll see you."

Margaret should have left it alone but her temper surged. "Where are you going, Dad?"

"The goddamn ballgame."

"John'll be here. Don't you think you ought to stay?"

"I don't want to see that asshole."

122

Jake, pained, shoving back into the couch, toes pointing in. "C'mon, Terrell, don't."

"Don't? Don't what?"

"Don't shit on it."

"Me? I'm shitting on you?" Terrell stalked out the back door. Margaret followed. She warned him to keep quiet but he cut her off with "I know, I know." Pacing, biting his lip, but he couldn't hold it. "He's the asshole! He's the one shit on him and you know it!"

Margaret went back in and shut the door on him. Jake's eyes were swimming. She started, "He just means—"

But Terrell rushed back through the door himself. Hat knocked back on his head. "I just meant—" Had to grab the floor as he squatted down in front of Jake, trying to hug his shoulder, loving him all wrong. "Jakey, I just meant, who the hell'd leave you? How could anybody leave a kid like you?"

Jake jerked past him, ran out of the room.

Margaret was furious at her father. The doorbell rang.

Jake's face—the light bursting through the studied non-chalance—seized both their hearts. Him looking at them like, Is this all right? Hands in pockets, bouncing along at his father's side, gingerly.

After they'd left, Margaret was the one to glare. "See, Dad? It doesn't matter what you feel about this. What—"

"Don't tell me See." Terrell shaded his eyes. "I see."

Not so long ago.

"If I knew where I went during those spells," Terrell said then, "I'd let you in on it. But I don't remember a goddamn thing."

"You're in there, Terrell," Jake yawned. "You just book for a while."

With a dig of his polished shoe, Terrell set the swing going. He said, "Jakey, Margaret," a new bleakness to his voice. Jake, who'd been dumping out his coffee into the grass, looked up sharply.

WHEN THEY GET up to the ICU and ring the buzzer, Jake and Margaret are not admitted. "We're getting him comfortable," the voice on the intercom says.

They lean against another wall. The ICU waiting room is full, tables littered with styrofoam cups, soft drink cans on the beige carpet. A pay phone rings; someone answers, calls out McFaddin! A woman in jeans claims the phone, covers her mouth, whispering into it.

Margaret takes off her glasses, needed for signing the papers, snaps them into their case. *Oh Dad*, she says, talking to Terrell in her mind. Two people in ER greens and stethoscopes run down the hall.

Margaret stalks over to the buzzer, pushes again. "I want to come in," she raises her voice. "I want to be with my father."

"Comfortable, comfortable," the voice says.

Jake shifts over as Margaret returns to the wall and slips down it, crouched now on her haunches, oblivious to the skirt, the pumps. Her fingertips push against her lips as she takes in the scene around her. The light is strange up here, devoid of ER brightness. There are shadows in the middle of it, shadows in the hall that people walk through. The talk from the waiting room is hushed, as though to be louder would disturb the ICU's desperately ill. Margaret doesn't want to cram herself in there with the other worried families, doesn't consider going in. She feels strongest crouched here, elbows on her knees, wound-up, ready. A lot of dark light pooled under the fluorescents enters into her. It is in this position—hunkering, her body's surface reduced and protected but also balanced, gathered—that she finally lets herself understand Terrell may be dying. Right now, on the other side of that door.

She springs up and mashes the buzzer; she does not let up. This time, no one answers. Margaret kicks the door with her business pump. "Mom," Jake protests, self-conscious that passersby have turned in the hallway to look at her. The muted chatter of the waiting room has ceased; heads have poked out.

After a few more kicks—Jake's got her by the elbow now—the door opens and a nurse, a small Oriental woman in rimless glasses, says Terrell's name, admits Jake and Margaret. "What number?" Margaret presses, seeing a line of glassed-in rooms, orange numbers painted by the doors.

"Three. But please." The nurse ushers them neatly into an unused side room, flips on the light, opens her mouth. *Oh no* is wrenched out of Margaret, along with her breath. Diversion into the side room has told her everything. But Jake's eyes fasten on her, large, alarmed.

"What?" he asks. "What?"

She sees he has kept himself far in reserve; nothing seems very real to him. "Oh Jakey," Margaret cries, setting the heels of her hands to her forehead.

"I'm afraid he didn't make it," the little nurse jumps in with it, gets it over with, conscientiously looking up into their faces. In a bizarre flash Margaret wonders if they have a rotation, a lineup, who delivers the news this time, is there a chart? But Jake advances on the nurse, a big kid with Terrell's imposing eyebrows, loudly bewildered.

"But my mother was asking to get in here. Why didn't you let her in?"

The nurse ebbs back on tiny feet. A knot of nurses appears and blocks the doorway; ostensibly to support their coworker against Jake, who, following Margaret as she pushes through them, searches each nurse's face, demands personally of each, "What's wrong with you? Why did you bullshit us? What's wrong with this place?"

In each darkened room a huge cylinder, a silver trunk sprouting monitors and wires grows out of the floor behind the beds. The faces on the pillows are old and strained.

Room #3 has the same cylinder but the face on the pillow is covered with a towel that Margaret knows instantly was not placed but tossed. She shuts the door behind them. Terrell is still connected to the machines, to monitors with red and green lights. He is propped up, just as he was in the

ER but his arms are thrown out, both of them awful, bloody halfway to the wrists, his clean palms curled open. One knee is cocked up, as if Terrell had been gathering leverage to leap out of the bed. Margaret removes the towel from his face. His teeth clench a black plug like a whistle; his eyes are half open. He doesn't look at her. Margaret rounds the bed once, again, but no matter where she's standing, her father looks some place else.

The floor floats up to her knees; her father's wrist meets her forehead; both her hands lock on his arm. Behind her squeezed eyes tumble blocks of red and green and black and yellow, shattering into her head. She's crying but it doesn't feel like that; she's shut off from the sound. What she feels is a deep and frictionless pouring—from her breastbone, her chest, her shoulders, her throat. Terrell's arm is somehow warmer than before, almost warm, she is so grateful for this, and she holds his arm, smoothing down the hairs again and again. "Dad," she's shaking her head. *Oh oh oh oh* comes out of her in rhythm with her rocking. For Margaret is rocking herself there on her knees, her nose running, absorbing pictures—Terrell's rages blindnesses unwisdom need, and Terrell's fierce love—the moments of her father's life flash simultaneously on a dark screen. None seems more than another. Rocking, she takes in the whole of Terrell's life and after what she cannot tell is a long time or any recognizable time at all her shoulders are grazed, a tentative effort at comfort made.

Jake—she has not forgotten Jake but left him to his own. Margaret struggles to come back, to focus on her son. She pulls herself to her feet but she cannot gather herself. She has a responsibility here; what can she say? He's not in there anymore, Jakey. That body is not him. He's in a better place.

No. That's not at all how it feels to Margaret. Terrell is here in this room with the people who love him. He is the one now who seems solid, real, while Margaret cannot consolidate herself. Down on her knees inside of Terrell's life, she allowed the molecules of her body to diffuse; she joined the room's dimness.

What Margaret says is: "Are you scared, Jake? You don't have to stay here anymore. I need to be here a while with him but you can leave. You can go—"

Jake jerks his head from side to side, refusing. His fists ram into his pockets. "Look at him," he whispers, the whisper all twisted. "They've like trashed him." Jake's face mashes in as he waves at Terrell's disarray—the messy hair, the crusted mouth with the black plug still inserted, the white stubble, the arms.

Margaret recognizes in her son's charge the Terrell opposition: lone, bare-knuckled fighter vs. powers-that-be. Given the casual refusal on the intercom, the towel tossed over her father's face, she can't say she doesn't feel it herself. She surely does; she would not be Terrell's daughter if she didn't. But Terrell could not win this one. She raises a hand.

"They were trying to save him," she tells her son, as a nurse with a badge, her face creased in sympathy, enters with a chair for Margaret; the room has no chairs. Jake takes charge of it, an orange, molded plastic thing so light it swings in his hand. "Please would you keep out of here now," he says.

The nurse—her badge signals some kind of rank—seems to want to talk to them but Margaret's glance instantly slides over her and returns to Jake. "Look, it all happens fast. It's not them against us."

"Yeah it is!" Jake stalks the narrow channel between the foot of the bed and the sink. "Did you see a doctor up here? Did he get a doctor?" He whirls around, backing the nurse toward the door. "Huh? How come one of you told us and not a doctor?"

"We do usually inform the families," she says. "It's standard. We're very sorry for your loss, believe me."

"How come you didn't let my mother be with him?"

"This was a code, honey. She wouldn't have been allowed in the room anyway, not during a code. Only—"

Jake's thick voice skids into hers. "She was out there kicking the door. How come you didn't let her in?"

The nurse's lips tighten in resignation though her eyes stay soft. Her hand rests on the door knob; she seeks out Margaret first. Then she gives Jake a clear look. "It's just how it's done," she says.

Jake tracks her out into the nurses' station. "But how come it's done?" he demands of her; his reined-in voice quivers with bitterness. He scans them all, demands that of everyone standing there. And they do stand there, frozen, one with a tray half-lifted.

"He had to die all by himself. Did you forget that? Did you even think of it? When you kept my mother out in the hall? How come that's the code—that you made him die all by himself? You know . . ." Jake's face crumples and he looks down and then up at them again. "You just shouldn't do this to anybody else. Not to anybody again."

Margaret flings her arms around him when he comes back in and they cry holding each other, their heaving shoulders knocking, for Terrell who died alone here in this room. When Jake pulls away, he tips his face as if to make his tears roll back into his eyes. "Man and they fucking trashed him," he whispers.

It's the arms Jake means, the poor bloody arms.

Margaret releases a long, shuddering sigh and drags a hand across her eyes. "All right," she says.

After some utterly static interval, she says it again: "All right."

She sets the chair against a wall, out of their way and walks back to the bed. She removes the black thing from Terrell's mouth. She drops it on the floor with the other debris; she hasn't noticed before how bits of tubing, paper packagings torn open, a plastic glove with the fingers poked in, gauze patches are strewn all over. Margaret peels off tape, pulls out needles, lets them dangle. Terrell's old suitcase is propped crookedly against the wall, as though a kick has landed it there. Jake watches her as she fetches it.

"Fix his knee, Jake."

He wipes his nose on his shoulder, and then does, laying both Terrell's legs straight. Margaret unsnaps the suitcase and sets the shaving kit in Jake's hands. "You're the man. You're the one that shaves. Do what you can," she shrugs.

Jake blinks at her and then stares down at the nicked brown leather.

Margaret roots around in the suitcase for something to wash with. She hears the kit's quick zipper, then, still picking through the underwear, the pajamas, hears the hiss and splut of the aerosol can. When she glances over, Jake is smoothing the creme on Terrell's face. He applies the creme in light dabs, as though Terrell might criticize.

Margaret pulls out a pajama top and goes over to the sink. She soaks one of Terrell's pajama sleeves clear through and wrings out the water. From the sink she can see through the plate glass window into the ICU station, where the nurses are walking around or making notes. One glances at her and down again. Margaret slips her hand inside the wet pajama sleeve. Then she comes back to the bed.

Jake, having willed her away or forgotten her presence, whichever he had to do, shaves Terrell with elaborately gentle strokes, one hand stroking, dipping to wipe the blade on a corner of sheet, the other hand hovering, guarding Terrell's face from hurt. Margaret watches just long enough to know she should turn away. If her son had a wife, she could watch but this intimacy isn't a mother's domain. Somehow he has entered into his own private tenderness, and is allowing his hands to be driven by that.

Margaret bends her head and starts to wash the thick bloodstains off Terrell's arms. The pajama sleeve is slick polyester with no absorbency but the washing calms her—scrubbing, walking over to rinse the cloth, scrubbing again. All sounds filter away, the tiny scrape of the razor, distant murmuring from outside, the air conditioner's whir. They work on in silence. Margaret's movements work into a stillness; stillness takes hold and spreads inside her. She washes her father's shoulders, his chest with the gray hairs, not so old, not an old bowed chest, visible strength remains. She has never touched her father this way. She brushes aside the sheet to wash his legs, his feet with the thick yellow toenails. All the washing is stillness.

When she looks up, Jake has finished the shaving; he's combed Terrell's hair. But distress marks his forehead. He asks her, "Is he like gonna freeze like this?"

Terrell's clean chin has nestled downward like a shamed boy's.

Jake throws the comb into the shaving kit, shoves it at Margaret. He clambers up into the bed beside Terrell and puts his hands under Terrell's chin, shoring it up.

Margaret backs blindly against the wall, to get her breath. That Jake would do this, that he didn't hesitate. He twists to look at her, sure and unsure, willing and aghast at himself. She swipes at her nose, flinching at the touch of the cold, wet pajama sleeve she forgot was there. "Oh God," Margaret finds herself laughing, "if he could see you." She flaps the sleeve toward Jake, who mumbles, "Weird." Slowly their faces change. They know it's not weird, it's natural to want to preserve Terrell's dignity. Dignity's what Terrell cared about. It doesn't seem their fault that everything is wrong and right at the same time.

"Just a minute, okay?" Margaret shakes off the sleeve and squats down to pack the kit away into the suitcase, telling Jake what she is going to do. Then she marches out the door to the nurses' station. She is about to ask for the number of Hostetter's Mortuary—the only familiar name she can think of; she went to high school with Jim Hostetter—when the nurse wearing the badge rushes to hand her a post-it with the three funeral home numbers jotted on it. The nurse is ready for this; she's been waiting. This must be what always happens at this point. Margaret uses the nurses' phone. She announces who and where she is to the man who answers, and who Terrell is, and that he is a friend of Mr. Hostetter, Sr.'s. Was a friend.

"Margaret?"

"Jim?" His professionally kind voice is repeating the name of the hospital; he already knows the ICU is located on the third floor.

Margaret says, "Jim, my father would hate to be seen with his chin falling in. My son is in there right now holding up his grandfather's chin."

Jim Hostetter says he can have someone there within the hour. Her son really doesn't have to do that.

Margaret replies he's already doing it and an hour is not so long.

A nurse excuses herself by Margaret without making eye contact. She must stand on tiptoe to examine a chart on the wall over Margaret's shoulder. On impulse, Margaret requests a broom and once the nurse, looking confused, finds her one, Margaret is relieved to get out of her territory. She opens the door, nodding at Jake so he knows arrangements are made. She's glad to reenter their own room. The room is Terrell's house. It is a place that belongs to them as long as he is here—to her and Terrell and Jake. She is not ready to leave it.

She sweeps up the debris on the floor, the torn-open packagings, the glove, the red-spotted gauze, the black plug, and makes a pile of it all for the wastebasket. Every so often grief folds her and then, hardly registering Jake next to him, she takes in Terrell, here, still here with them, and she breathes more easily. Margaret makes a rhythm with her sweeping, the rhythm Terrell's heart couldn't keep or the rhythm of stillness again, brushing and pulling back in soft strokes, around the cylinder, even into the corners, sweeping all the room. When she has finished—Margaret rubs her face with both hands; she has finished, hasn't she?—then brings the orange chair to the bed and sits down.

She doesn't want to do anything more, doesn't want to ask or tell anyone anything, she just has to be here, be in this gap, inside this mystery that broke open. Jake raises his head. They read one another's wet eyes, verifying this strange and terrible day.

Jake turns away and abruptly complains, "Mom."

Two nurses stare through the plate glass. In all her smoothing, Margaret had forgotten them, smoothed them, too, away from her and Jake and Terrell. For a moment, dully, she cannot imagine why the nurses stand there staring. What are they looking at? She turns her head to see what they see. Not her tender son. A fierce, rangy teenager cramped on a bed, naked knees poking through ragged jeans, cupping an old man's chin. An old code they lost, with that vacant gaze they see every day up here.

"Get them out of there, Mom." Jake's voice rises, threatening, but Margaret exclaims, "Jakey, wait."

She'll draw the curtain shortly; the nurses are already skittering off to charts and trays. First Margaret protects her father from anyone's intrusion. She closes his eyes. "Now," she says, holding down the lid of one with her fingertips, holding the other with the heel of her hand. She doesn't know who she's talking to. She doesn't even know if the eyes will stay closed or not. All she knows is that it's her place to do it. Instant by instant she's learning her new place. She has to; Jake's watching. He will remember everything she does.

# The Plains
# of Xanadon

I FINISHED THE scene where I-Bork excites the genotypes to rebel with him against the Regime and skimmed right through the next—their plea to join the outlaws of the stronghold. I was charged, soothed, drops of sweat rolled down my ribs; I was in love with making, and making things up. When the phone rang again, I did not bother with Hello.

"I did mean it, Isaac. It's over. This just hurts both of us," I said.

A silence. Then Mr. Tottenham, Kevin to no one, announced himself by saying he was sorry but he was not Isaac, or perhaps in the circumstances one might infer, he was not sorry. English clearing of throat. In any event he was calling to inquire if it might be convenient for me to work an extra shift at The Olde Pub since business this evening was so very brisk.

"How brisk?" I heard clinking, a solid roar of voices.

"Middling. No, perhaps quite. Middling to quite brisk."

A distant but dazzling smash of water glasses going down for the last time—some rude clapping. I waited, phone mashed between shoulder and cheek, fingers on the keys.

"Hell. Okay, Althea," Mr. Tottenham switched to the American dialect we speak here in Houston. "Oil and Gas Convention. The waiters are slammed. Knee deep. They are in the trees."

"Weeds, in the weeds," I corrected.

"Right. May we count you in?"

I skipped down and typed:

*11 - INT PALACE - EVENING*
*ALANNA (dressed in spy garb) enters the palace of the Regime.*

I laid my forehead briefly on the typewriter; inspiration is everywhere. Then I retrieved my work clothes from under the bed and swiped an iron across them.


DEPENDING ON WHO you are, you might look at me and think Cheap or Exploited; I would probably agree I look both—but that is my wench suit. I'd add Silly because that's my opinion of the costume The Olde Pub furnishes: lowcut white blouse, blacklaced waist-cincher over a tiny red skirt with matching panties. I buy my own fishnet stockings, wear my own black heels; sometimes my hips bulge because I've loaded my pockets with croutons from the salad bar.

I used to want to drop a trail of croutons into the parking lot and disappear; to lie down in a flowery meadow and sleep for a year and wake up with some dark-haired sexy guy kneeling down to me. Since those things never happened, I decided to rescue myself and not ask where I was taking me.

So in my screenplay—fantasy abounds! I've made most everyone at the restaurant a character, stealing for myself, more or less, their real names:

Cast

Rupert, busboy ................. RUPIN, Outlaw Captain

Lourdes, dishwasher ............ LOURN, Outlaw Captain

Dennis, bartender ............... DENNISIAN,
                                   Hermaphrodite informer

Vinh, Vietnamese waiter ..... VYNN,
                                   shaman of ritual dances

Althea (me) .......................... ALANNA, spy etc. etc.

Alanna is much wiser than me, Althea. She does not have a boyfriend like the one I am trying to shed, silver-tongued Isaac, whom I've called I-Bork, and patterned after himself and after the raccoons that used to raid my mother's old refrigerator in the garage. These were small and nasty though clever in surprising ways, and they were adorable to look at. In my screenplay, I-Bork and his like genotypes are minor characters, a blundering band of counter-outlaws who often behave like raccoons.

For example. In their first big scene, set, like all the others, on the planet Xanadon, I-Bork and his genotypes appear at the Stronghold pleading to join the Outlaws in their war against the Regime. The visit does not go as they'd hoped. Why not? Because it never does.

The genotypes, who include Rout, a bearish henchman modeled on Isaac's best friend Robert, have been led outside to wait while I-Bork argues their case. The Outlaws laugh at him. They are not more than normally cruel. If you saw him on the wide screen—diminutive, orange-complected, ring-tailed—you would laugh, too. But I-Bork makes an impassioned speech. Yes, he agrees, his kind are small and striped but in order to fight, "Do we have to look just like you? Do you think we don't laugh or weep as you do? We don't bleed?" I-Bork's squinty eyes blaze.

Unfortunately for him, the genotypes, shut out of the

meeting, get bored and dart into the kitchen to dip their paws into the cold stew. Their cohort Rout tries to dissuade them but is entranced by the sight of a pretty cook carrying a tray of radish roses with cinnamon paste. Alanna, a spy for the outlaw legions, is changing her rough clothes for the flashier ones worn in the Regime household she infiltrates when she is drawn by the noise. She finds the kitchen disrupted and Rout lumbering after the cook, his snout smeared with cinnamon.

Alanna throws open Captain Rupin's door just as I-Bork, shadowed by the tall Outlaws, crescendoes his speech: "We've always been your allies. You just don't look down far enough to see us!"

His fervent conviction might have moved the Outlaws, even veteran captains like Rupin and Lourn. We all lust to be moved. But the disheveled genotypes tumble in at the height of their leader's eloquence; I-Bork's face crumples with humiliation. Captain Lourn, disgusted, tosses her stit-gun to Rupin, suggesting he do the planet a favor and shoot the genotypes' noses off. Everyone looks toward Vynn, the Outlaw Shaman with the jeweled forehead. He nods No. I give Alanna the last line. "Yeah, Rupin," she says. "They can't help sabotaging themselves, they live for it. Let them go."

So I-Bork and his genotypes are ejected from the north gate of the Stronghold, while from the south gate the camera follows a discouraged Alanna. Glancing behind her, she slips out of the Stronghold. She drudges along, kicking pebbles from her way, but soon her pace picks up. Pan to a beautiful landscape with deep golden light and blue shadows of evening. Huge trees near a turn of river, mountain peaks rimmed with moonglow. Alanna's small figure whirls round and round, gives a little leap, continues walking.

End of scene.

Not exciting? No blood sacrifice, no explosions? I will get to those eventually. *The Screenwriters' Bible* tells me first works tend to be autobiographical. So I'll admit I've passed on to Alanna my own peculiar vulnerability: I believe with all my heart it is possible to love people without killing them.

But do my hero Alanna's actions, there at the end, speak? The *SB* warns that scripts do have practical boundaries beyond which other elements prevail. I need: 1.) a closeup of her face 2.) a skillful actress to capture the spirit within the physical movements. Alanna sheds the draining scene behind her by taking in the light and the mountains; she winds herself in the beauty of the evening. It is a simple restoration of her bounty. For even Alanna, a mere spy, has bounty—constantly being used up and replenished. On this particular evening, it wells up in her like tears well up but if you felt it fill her you would know it as joy.

THE WAITERS were indeed in the weeds. Even the busboy had been sucked in as a helper. Rupert's feather was bedraggled; his eyes, normally omniscient, were hooded. "Slow it down, white girl," he murmured when I hurried at him in the hall, my little tray crowded with tall Tom Collinses. He drifted past with a gravy boat of mushrooms just as Vinh darted by clutching a bottle of yellow wine. "Pardon pardon," Vinh sang out. Rupert and I had to hug the wall. "Damn," he said; mushroom juice had dripped onto his tunic.

I nudged Rupert's elbow. "Listen, he's speaking it."

Vinh gabbled happily to the couple at 14—a bearded man and his wife, whose blonde hair looked tossed rather than combed. While the bearded man swirled, sipped, and inclined his head to the side, Vinh cradled the wine bottle, gazing down on it tenderly.

Rupert was speculative. "Talking French change that little mother's personality for the better. Now how come?"

"The French had Vietnam before we got stuck with it. Vinh must have taken to them."

Rupert nodded. The tip of the scar on his chest stuck out

above his squire's tunic. It was shaped like a fern. "He be homesick for some place he never been."

Rupert's face got dreamy the way it never did around another male, the way it does sometimes when I put him by a campfire out on the starry plains of Xanadon. I asked him if he'd like to see Africa someday.

"Yeah I would," he said.

Bouncing, Tottenham led a party of six to their dark table. He'd made the mistake of confiding to Dennis, our snitch bartender, that whenever the restaurant was busy he felt "rather an American success story." Dennis had imitated him blushing. Tottenham dusted his hands at us. "Chop chop," he said jauntily.

Rupert studied him, then sailed away to deliver the mushrooms.

I didn't get a lull until nine o'clock, then I loaded my pockets with croutons and inhaled them in the kitchen. I was about to turn back toward the black sucking tunnel of the hall when Lourdes made some Argentinean disapproval noises and slouched out from behind the Hobart. A sharp-boned, sinewy little tough with a boy haircut, she pinched my cheeks together so she could brush off my face. This would have made me feel funny if she hadn't been so rough about it. What a grip. Lourdes and I tried to speak each other's languages so when she let go of my jaw, I accused her in my Tex-Mex Spanish.

"Creo que tu estás mas grande, chica": Girl, I thought you were bigger.

Barricaded behind the Hobart dishwashing equipment Lourdes projected enormousness, a device to aid her constant skirmishes with the cooks. Closeup, though, my eyes were taller than hers. She shot a glance at the cooks who, spatulas and meatforks poised, were frankly staring at us. One of them tilted his eyebrows at me and growled something in puro mexicano to Lourdes; they all tittered. She fired them a violent, complicated, and immediately comprehensible hand sign. Noisily the cooks pretended fear.

Lourdes tapped her collarbone. "Que viva yo," she said, her teeth showing. Long live me. The cooks, with one exception, were delighted to respond with Mexican lipmusic. The exception was an undercook the others called Muy; his real name was Persian and harder to pronounce. He'd once worked twenty-two shifts straight, got all bearded and hollow-eyed, then believed his selflessness on behalf of The Olde Pub entitled him to squeeze the waitresses' breasts. Muy gazed at Lourdes savagely, the muscles of his face contracting.

"Fanático," she dismissed him, smiled, and strolled back to her territory. Muy lunged toward her but the salad man frowned and impatiently waved him back.

Rupert lumbered by me with his buscart. "I sposed to tell you . . ." His index finger tipped toward the hall, so I followed him. "I got a important message—" Rupert stopped, raising his chin toward one of the tables: Vinh was being tortured.

A table of drunk conventioneers was calling him *gook* and *chink*. Blank-faced, his eyebrows delicately arched, Vinh spun about collecting dirty plates, replacing knives they'd dropped. The men wanted to know *hey gook* what he could see out that third eye—Vinh had a mole, a ruby red one, between his eyebrows. He circled the table, pivoting, swiveling, dodging between them, keeping out of their reach. Then one man caught hold of his costume sword. Vinh's momentum continued, and a plate flew out of his hand onto the faux-flagstone congoleum and bounced. The men exploded laughing.

Rupert said, "Damn." Poor Vinh looked like a hummingbird trapped by its tail.

Rupert rolled his buscart like a tumbril up to the table. He leaned between Vinh and the man who'd caught him, said "Scuse me," and jerked the man's plate away. Vinh fluttered free. Rupert picked up the plate on the floor and then the others, stacking them into a pile. Some of the men edged back to let him work.

139

"Where'd you get that scar?" the one who'd captured Vinh asked him.

The scar tip showed charcoal on Rupert's brown skin, its curved stem thickening as it descended into his tunic. Stitchmarks leafed out from it. Rupert's mouth mashed in briefly. "Ain't important."

"Some kind a surgery?"

The corners of Rupert's lips curled up.

The man laughed. "So what do you call important, son?"

"That it all on my *forward side*." Looking straight at him, Rupert flicked his wrist and broke the last plate *crash* against the pile.

I felt a thrill of satisfaction, a small but appreciable counter-force. This is why I have made Rupert a captain. He may not defeat the Regime but he neutralizes, in guerilla fashion, the occasional Regime offense. In Houston, Texas, in the year 1976, Rupert Hill may be a busboy, but in 2114 he is an outlaw captain on the plains of Xanadon.

Back out in the hall, I smiled at him. Rupert looked at me.

Tottenham glowered into the bus tub. "More breakage?"

"Man these plates weak," Rupert said.

Ticking his fingers, Tottenham ran down case prices of simulated Elizabethan stoneware until a cook semaphoring with a carrot caught his attention.

When he dashed off, Rupert looked after him impassively. Then his eyes cut toward me and away. "I sposed to tell you your brother out back."

My buoyance evaporated. My brother bosses a rig off the coast of New Guinea. It was either Isaac out there, or his best friend, his sad-eyed emissary, Robert the kind and bumbling. Neither way would I go back there and see.

I retreated to my station in the bar where Dennis had just popped in the Greensleeves tape Mr. Tottenham considered posh. Dennis entertained the usual admirers. Lovelorn Greg, an architect with shepherd boy curls, sketched buttresses on his napkin, hoping for a word. "Al?" he whispered as I passed, his face a ruin of grief. "There's no one that I know of," I patted Greg, the operative word being *one*.

"Except her. She was here last week, too," Greg glared toward the south end of the bar where the wine lady sat. He checked his watch. "She usually gives up by now."

Between them, Dennis basked in the bar's advantageous pink light, arching his back as he ran fingers through already tousled blond hair. He managed to give the impression the top button of his jeans was always open. When he reached for the Chablis to pour the wine lady's fourth glass of white, he presented his profile. Long lashes shadowed the cheekbone, the flawless complexion; his eyeliner was expertly smudged.

"She doesn't even talk to him," I assured Greg.

"Talking's not what she's interested in." Greg slashed his pencil through a buttress, then rested the eraser on his forehead. "Oh listen. I hate me. I'm such a shit."

At the bar's other end, the wine lady sipped Chablis. She had on a pretty bias-cut dress, 30's or 40's, something you find secondhand if you really have an eye. She held herself aloof from us but I was rooting for her to win Dennis anyway; I liked Greg.

I started when Rupert slid next to me with five platters of bones stacked on his arm. "Your brother say this problem is bad. He need you to help him and he gettin mildewed out there . . ."

"Tell him to please go home. You know that's not my brother back there, don't you?"

Rupert snorted in scorn. He doesn't answer rhetorical questions, anyway.

"What brother? I thought your brother was in Borneo. Or somewhere." Dennis pretended to rinse a highball glass, but he was eavesdropping, trolling for tidbits. When he does this on Xanadon, he slips away soon after and appears through a velvet side curtain into the palace of the Regime.

"Why is your brother lurking around out back?"

"Quarantine."

Dennis's gorgeous eyes got large. They were violet, like Elizabeth Taylor's.

Greg slid off the bar stool as I went by. "I'm going to hack a century off my sentence in purgatory." He went over, hopped on the stool by the wine lady, and stuck out his hand. Her fingertips grazed his palm and retracted.

I took orders from some secretaries who'd slipped their high-heels off under the table, and from two refinery types who would be made uncomfortable by Mr. Tottenham as soon as he detected their presence. While I waited for Dennis to mix up strawberry daiquiris, Greg tried to build a conversation with the wine lady. He seemed obsessively earnest. He introduced himself; she flexed her lips. He complimented her dress; she dipped her head. He described his job and asked the wine lady about hers. She shrugged. He threw a desperate look over his shoulder but I deserted to serve my tables. Tottenham had already zeroed in on the two sweatstained refinery workers with black creased into their hands. He was being so jovially British to them they would never come back.

When I docked at the bar again, Greg sagged on his stool, reduced to asking the wine lady if she'd been in Houston long. She indicated No. She blew some smoke not quite away from him.

Dennis stood back in the pink light, blissed out.

Greg lowered his curly head. "Look, I thought we could at least be civilized." His little shepherd face burned vermillion in patches. "No. Let me be really stupid. I had this bizarre, pathetic fantasy that we might acknowledge our competition, you know, chat up a little camraderie . . ."

She watched him with a crease between her soft brown eyebrows.

". . . so when Dennis chose one of us the other might not feel so bad because we'd developed a kind of . . . team spirit. Oh, right!" Greg thumped his temple, stuck out his tongue, and bobbed his head like a dummy. "Go ahead, ridicule me, sweetheart, let it out. Then I'll skulk back to my corner and we'll do the same old cutthroat number."

The wine lady was staring at Greg, stricken. Her cigarette had burned out at the filter.

"I mean, you didn't even have the grace to tell me your name. Just sat there like a mute while I beat my tiny misguided brains out trying to talk to you."

Her fingers crept over to his fist. She opened her mouth. Nothing came out.

The wine lady tried again, her brow strained. We waited. She chewed away at the air. Greg sat absolutely still except for his eyelids, strobe-blinking in misery. When she finally produced sound, it was the most brutal stutter you could imagine. It took her a couple of minutes to tell Greg her name was Callie and she thought his fantasy was stupid but also the loveliest thing she'd ever heard. Greg put his head down *thunk* on the bar.

You could see Dennis's self-image as a sensitive human being get a choke-hold on his desire to fall down laughing. He made some stifled noises then, irritable, confronted me. "This business about your brother being quarantined, Al."

"What about it?"

"I know you're making fun of me," he said. The violet beauties grew very small. He asked me to go out to the kitchen and get a jar of pearl onions for Gibson martinis, the kind of errand I often did.

"No."

He turned a coquettish ear to me. "I'm sorry. What?"

"I don't want to go back there."

"Al. You have to, I said." He grinned, slowly.

"Nuh uh."

Dennis flounced out of the bar. In forty seconds Mr. Tottenham was behind me. "Onions, Althea," he pointed toward the hall.

I trudged out of the bar through the tunnel, and put my

hands up to ward off the harsh kitchen lights. You could barely hear the low radio they were working to—no Greensleeves back here. Conjunto, ayyyiyiyiiii. The cooks were almost out of the weeds, since the kitchen closed at ten, but they were still heads down, elbows flying, chinga this, gimme the chingado that. The salad man was knocking back the dinner salads and singing into a paring knife. When someone tipped the radio over and killed the music, the whole kitchen groaned. More chingas; the radio was helped to its feet again. Muy took a kick to the butt. He whirled on the kicker but in the combined glow of eight Mexican eyes subsided with a sickly smile.

I peered in at Lourdes. "Oye, guapa, any news from Buenos Aires?" Lourdes hated to be called Pretty but she was, sort of, if she wasn't looking at you.

I wished she wasn't looking at me now. As she nodded her head, I heard a bell toll. She'd been telling me people in her country were just disappearing off the streets. "Un vecino," she whispered, a neighbor who lived around the corner, a young man, was gone. "Mi familia . . . they don see him. Nada mas." Lourdes passed her wet hands through the air.

"Where do you think he went?"

"To the devil's office."

I could hardly hear her. "Where is that?"

"How nice you don't know."

I waited, but she didn't say anything more. "Y tu famila? What do they think about all this?"

"They think . . ." She closed her eyes for a time before she finished the sentence. Mostly, she told me, they thought about her sister Rosa, who was soon to be married. Rosa, who had long black hair like mine. Lourdes shrugged but something in her face lightened a little, anyway.

"Bueno hombre?"

Lourdes snuffled loudly so I understood she thought the groom a pig.

144

"Dígame, chica," I leaned against the stainless steel, wetting my red skirt, "don't you know one good man in Buenos Aires?"

Lourdes leaned out of range of the old steno chair she kept behind the Hobart and spit on the floor. "Buenos Aires," she growled, "the Silver City." Except she pronounced it Silver Shitty. I smiled. She narrowed her eyes. "Eh?" she said.

"City," I said, "Lourdes, say city."

"See-ty," she threatened, like it meant machete.

I made my face bland but she hissed "seet-y," like this time it meant tiny boy scout knife, her mouth puckered with insecurity. This made me laugh though it was possible to invite violence by correcting an alien's pronunciation. Lourdes stood back projecting enormousness then gave it up, flipped down a cigarette from behind her ear, and lit it.

"Mira," I said. "I do believe what you've been telling me. That people disappear from Buenos Aires." I said, or meant to say, that she was describing a terrible thing—that these people were not innocently zipping away in cars, planes, or catching busses.

"Que?" she asked, in disbelief.

"Busses," I repeated, " los Greyhound, sabes, gente cogen los busses."

I thought she was barking at me. She had to sit down in the steno chair because she was making that sound which turned out to be Argentinean laughing.

Now I felt sullen. "What?" I asked her. "What did I say?"

In Spanish she told me, "You said a truth. But stupidly." Lourdes spit on her fingers, pinched her cigarette out, and dropped the butt in her pocket. She made a circle with thumb and forefinger and jabbed her other index finger in and out of the circle. Apparently I had used the crudest of verbs to inform her people in Buenos Aires mate with Greyhound busses. "I like you," Lourdes told me, using that funny vos with the you familiar, the "you" you use with friends.

"Ditto," I said, but she didn't get it so I told her I liked her too and asked her why she persisted in riling the cooks.

Lourdes wiped her hands on her white, stained pants. "Porque . . ." She reached out, her brow furrowed. ". . . because," she said, "I can't afford to lose my nerve." She plucked a strand of hair from my cheek with such slow and tender seriousness she unmoored me from time and place and sex and I almost kissed her skinned knuckles. She froze, but the abrupt movement at the corner of our eyes turned out to be Rupert.

Rupert skimmed by with a new box of steak knives from the storeroom. "Your brother say the problem is deterioratin and any minute now—"

Vinh barged between us and disappeared into the walkin.

Rupert rattled the knives. "That little—"

"Who helped his butt out tonight?"

Rupert's gaze rested on me, heavy with power. "May be. But that little mother need him some manners." Rupert swiveled and departed.

I went over to the walkin just as Vinh backed out of it. He had a plate of cheesecake slathered with blueberries in a blue sugar soup; his lip was curled in distaste. He jumped when he saw me. "Oo you have scareded me," he exclaimed. "You sneaky."

"Sorry."

Then he stiffened. His head jerked slightly in the direction of the back door. The mole was like a red caste mark; his eyes were pools of calm.

"I know. Rupert already told me my brother was out there."

"Brotha." Vinh giggled unhappily. "Your brotha."

It occurred to me I was a horrible, unworthy escapist: I didn't know where Vinh lived or if he had any relatives but I could describe precisely his dwelling on the snowy mountain of Kai—a pavillion of hand-fit fir looking down on the plains. As Vynn he owns the ancient texts, mask-making tools, stones, seashells, and feathers, a tea set painted with dylly-flowers, ankle bells for the ritual dances, an astonishingly fine tape player. Glancing toward the back door, I leaned against the wall and asked Vinh about his family.

"Have sista," Vinh said. "Auntie."

"What about your mother and father?"

All expression deserted Vinh's face. "Fa fa away."

"You were great with those assholes tonight. You didn't let them get to you."

"Pardon?"

"I mean those men at table 16."

Vinh's eyebrows brushed upward once, a bird's wingstroke. "Ah. Sisteen. Les conards."

"What?"

He sat down on some lettuce crates and invited me beside him. His lively fingertips encouraged me to repeat.

"I'll say it wrong."

"Oh no. You get." Vinh's eyes were so bright and sure. As though he knew me.

"Okay, Lez kooonarr," I mimicked.

"Bien. Très Français."

"Really?" I smiled.

"Oui. Alors. Les salauds."

"Lez sal-oh."

"Les emmerdeurs."

"Lez what?"

"Les emmerdeurs."

"Lezamerdurs."

"Très bien!" He sat back, bits of escaping lettuce like green trim frilling about his stockinged calves. His eyes were proud for me. I was proud for me.

"What do those mean?"

Vinh's index finger wagged.

I laughed. Of course, very bad words. "What a teacher you are," I said.

Vinh laid his hand on his knight's crest, directly over his heart. "Sank you." He laced his hands tightly. "My English bad." He strangled the consonants between En and ish. His lips folded tight. "But I get. Not want bottom life." For a second Vinh's face was fierce with dreams; it was a pretty sight.

"Could you go back to Vietnam and be a teacher?"

He shook his head vigorously.

"But what about your—?" Oh, dumb, dumb, I shut up about his parents but not in time.

Vinh's eyes grew distant and dry. "Nevva go back."

That ended our conversation. He stood up from the lettuce crates and held out his hand. "Come. Teach again."

Vinh unbuckled his sword, opened his arms, and lilted his head to invisible music. He began to conduct a waltz, breathing un deux trois, un deux trois. Un—he showed me—step out to the side, hold the beat. On the deux trois, rise tiptoe.

"Wait I don't . . . Wait!"

But Vinh launched us out, commandeering the floor, the circle path around the salad table. The salad man and his paring knife withdrew to the cooks, who ceased for the moment to cook. Vinh hummed, he counted; he closed his sad dry eyes. His red mole glowed like a ruby—I saw the perfection of the reflecting pool before the Taj Mahal, the shrine of living water. By and by we revolved, our ball change lighter than bubbles. If you watched us, you would think our feet were not touching sticky kitchen tiles—you would think we were absolved from touching.

But that was not the case.

Vinh was regenerating for himself a modicum of bounty. This dance was his miniscule repair. We restore ourselves, we restore the world; it is, he was showing me, our different degrees of proficiency which make us what we are. Vinh's commands were spare, melodic. Un deux . . . attention! we must not collide with Tott—

Tottenham strode directly to us, forehead creased. He jerked his thumb over his shoulder. Vinh leapt out of my arms, collected the cheesecake, and, swordless, flitted away. Tottenham headed him off and began admonishing him, rounding his words into Vinh's abject face.

"Altea." My wrist was seized by a clammy hand. "Vos no te vayas por afuera," Lourdes said, her chin jutting toward the back door.

It's okay, I told her. No es el policia. In America the police use the front door.

To which, as near as I could make out, Lourdes responded, It's an equal disaster.

She spoke rapidly, punctuating with lots of eh's. Her face was expressionless but her thumb pressed my arm each time she said eh? If I didn't respond, she stared into my face until I said "Si, I got it."

Lourdes kept starting sentences with "Si ellos . . ." If they. She used the verb "to resist" repeatedly, sometimes with "no" in front of it.

"If they . . . you resist, eh?"

"Si."

"If they . . . you don't resist, eh?"

"Si." I understood I was being given precise instructions but I couldn't catch her fast Spanish. The body language I could follow: Lourdes' olive face sallow in the kitchen light, dark eyes jumping from hallway to me to beyond, thumb on my forearm like a second pulse eh? eh?

"Yeah yeah," I said.

When she saw Mr. Tottenham bearing down, she let go of my wrist and slipped back behind the Hobart.

Mr. Tottenham planted himself in front of me. "Althea. We in the bar have waited breathlessly for news of you. Haven't come into contact with any of those nasty little onions? Brutes, aren't they, so dreadfully difficult to capture."

"I'm getting them. And I did serve everybody in the bar, Mr. Tottenham."

"Yes. Some of them have been so thoughtless as to finish what you've served them. Let's rack our brains. What course might now be the most appropriate for the cocktail hostess?"

Though it took me to the very mouth of the back door, I walked to the timeclock, dunked my timecard, and reslotted it. "Rest of the night's on me."

He had stalked behind me to the timeclock; when I turned I almost bumped into him. Defensively, I stuck my hands in my skirt pockets. Croutons. He was breathing on me. "That's generous but unnecessary, Althea, do you know you have a smashing figger."

"Figger?"

He took his glasses off and bowed his head to clean them. He was a lot younger than I'd thought, and his dark hair was almost as pretty as Dennis's—I suppose I had noticed that but filed it under Pass. Still, that the compliment seemed inadvertant bolstered my waning store of cheer.

"Thank you. Kevin."

His jaw softened. "Dennis has told me about your . . . you don't have to go out there, you know." He rushed off his coat, and began to roll up his sleeves. Briskly. "Any assistance I can—"

I had not put him on Xanadon before in any capacity; now I saw he was a captain, maybe a lieutenant. And suddenly—it was late, I was tired—I felt weary of captains with their counter-strike energy.

"I don't think I need you, Mr. Tottenham."

He looked at me, brow squeezed. Then his bottom lip shoved up and he put the coat back on. "Do excuse me. I meant to say it appears your job description has grown foggy in your memory. You are required to provide the bar with garnishes. You are required to tend to your customers' requests which obviously you cannot from the outer reaches of the kitchen—"

I opened the back door to a slit of dark. "Okay, Isaac, I give up. What do you want?"

A hand shot through and dragged me out.

I POUNDED HIM on the back of his neck.

"Look Al," Isaac hunched his shoulders against my blows, "we're through, okay? In the two or three lifetimes I waited out here, that message had time to penetrate my puny defense mechanisms, okay? But Robert's going to shoot himself. If he hasn't already. I need some fucking help."

"Oh no."

Isaac kept towing me to his car. "Oh yeah. He lifted the gun I lifted from my old man."

I dug my high heels in the tarmac to understand this; I liked his best friend Robert. "Why?"

Isaac turned around and stared at my wench clothes. "Man, you are got up like a French whore." The security lamp on the phone pole colored Isaac's face and ponytail orange. "I never get tired of it."

Isaac herded me into the back seat with Robert and then slid behind the wheel. Robert righted himself, pulling his legs back. "Hi, Al," he said. He had in one hand what looked like a dull metal water pistol with no white plastic plug to hold the water in. A foreign word appeared in my mind: schnauzer.

"Just look at you. All that black hair, that puffy white blouse, you look like Snow White."

"Except the dwarves cut her skirt off," Isaac said, fishing over into the back seat.

I glared at Isaac until I saw he was actually trying to pick up the bourbon bottle by Robert without him noticing. Robert's hand snaked around to clutch the bottle. Together they managed to knock it over.

Robert retrieved it and scooched back on the seat. He was a big guy with red hair and freckles. He always dressed in ironed jeans and long-sleeved shirts he rolled up to the elbow, snappy clean, starched, like a palace lieutenant who's been serving the Regime a long, long time.

That's what he had on now, khakis and a sky-blue button-down but his feet were bare. A trickle of liquor gleamed on his chin. "So how's the movie going, Al?"

"It's going. Let Isaac have the gun and I'll tell you about it."

Robert stuck the pistol in his pants and held up both his hands. "Look Ma no gun. So am I in it?"

"Yeah you are. I made you look like a bear and you're in Isaac's band of outlaws."

"Hey neat. Do I get the girl?"

"As a matter of fact."

Robert clasped his hands over his head like a boxer. "All right! What does she look like?"

"She's a wonderful cook."

"That's what we want to hear! Does Isaac get a girl?"

"No. Isaac's tribal responsibilities require a vow of celibacy."

Robert pointed his finger at Isaac, laughing. Isaac banged the wheel. "So what're you, like the queen of something?" he asked.

"A spy."

"Like you get to fuck all the German officers, it's your job?" Slit-eyed, Isaac folded his arms.

"This is another world, Isaac, another cosmos, there's no Germany."

"Metaphorically speaking," Isaac said, and leaned against the window.

"Metaphorically speaking, right you are, whoever I want to," I said.

Isaac snapped up straight. "Like that English dickhead that answers the phone?"

"Guys, guys," Robert said. "My true pals." He raised his hands, peacemaking. "Al. I got a job offer."

Robert had stuck with school; he was about to graduate in some kind of engineering. I said, "But that's great, doing what?"

"Management, out of Sydney office. Keep the rigs humming. 45K to start."

"That's what my brother does, Robert, he goes all over. So what is this about?"

Isaac had turned back to the wheel.

"Al. Listen to this. They could have sent me anywhere. Saudi. Sicily. The Andes. New Jersey."

"My brother got war pay for Angola, he's rich. So what's the problem here? If you don't like Sydney, do your stint and transfer. Go somewhere else." Again I glanced over to the front seat for backup from Isaac, who gazed out the windshield like he had to pay attention to his driving.

"No, Al." Robert ran his finger around the mouth of the bottle. His voice was overly patient, sleepy, eerie.

"Al. When I was little that was just where I wanted to go. Australia. I made a map of it out of salt once and painted it green and brown. I pinned up the brim of my dad's fishing hat on one side. All eighth grade I talked with an Australian accent, mate. Of all the places in the world I wanted to go there. I planned it. You could say it was my heart's desire." Robert glugged a long swallow of the bourbon like it was tap water. "I guess I would say that now."

We were quiet. There was a connection missing here. Finally Robert saw I wasn't going to ask and I wasn't because the hairs on the back of my neck were rising.

"Mother says I should stay here and take a job out at Texaco whatever I can get. Stick nearby. For however long."

The hairs crawled. "However long what?"

Isaac spoke into the wheel. "Timmy's having a few minor heart problems."

I touched my forehead. I should have known it was Timmy—with Robert, it was always Timmy. He was Robert's twin brother, born with Down's syndrome. In some weird permutation Isaac understood but I had never followed, Robert's family blamed him for that. Not outright; they didn't actually say they blamed him—Isaac said they implied it in all kinds of covert ways. At the same time, they loved Timmy like crazy, this huge sweet child, and held it against Robert

153

that Timmy's natural life expectancy was short.

At "minor heart problems" Robert slumped back on the seat. His head hit the window and he grimaced but didn't say anything.

I took his hand but it slithered away from me. "Let me tell you something, Robert. Robert, take your hand off the dumb gun and look at me."

Robert propped his elbow up on the seatback in a sporty fashion. He glanced at me and away. His eyes were awful.

"Robert. When you and Timmy were floating around there in your mother's stomach—"

"Mother says I can't leave Timmy. He'd pine, for sure." Robert was cringing, this big man.

"Listen. You didn't hog all the brain tissue. You didn't take anything away from him or starve him out. Nothing you did made him what he is. Timmy was just born that way."

Tears rimmed Robert's eyes but did not fall out of them. "But we all love him that way. It's okay, Al, we wouldn't change Timmy now for—"

"All the tea in China." Which is what Isaac told me Robert's mother said all the time.

"Yeah, not for that, not for anything. Al—"

Timmy's red hair and freckles were just like Robert's. He was always smiling. The one time I'd seen him he was hugging Patsy, the family's golden retriever, and he told me he was going to marry her. His tilted almond eyes were incandescent with happiness. When Robert tried to leave, Timmy hugged him, and laid his cheek against his brother's chest. Robert must have done the same because now he said, "Timmy's heart is leaking. If you listen close, you can hear a whistle like a train coming."

Isaac groaned softly. I knew he was seeing Robert and Timmy—one big straight red-haired man and one short sloped red-haired man, body to body, listening to each others' hearts.

If he went away—how could Robert ever go away?—
Timmy would get worse and worse. They were 25 now. Some
day that train would burst into the station. "And what if I
wasn't there?" Robert frowned in disgust and poked his own
chest. "What if I was off in Australia?" He poked himself
roughly again.

Robert tried to slide off the seat and onto the car floor in
front of me. He hardly fit; his legs were bent and wedged in
down there and he leaned the heavy top half of himself on
me. But he seemed to have to be on the floor to tell me something, to get down really low. He put his hands on my knees
and then laid his forehead on his hands. "Al," he said, his
muffled voice vibrating, "let me tell you this terrible thing."

Isaac scratched furiously at a bugspot on the windshield
like he could chip it off from the inside. I looked down on
the back of Robert's thick bowed neck.

"Al, I still want to go. What do you think of that? I mean
what do you say to somebody like me?"

Robert's head came up. He leaned far away from me; I
thought he couldn't get me in focus. But he was just making
room; he hauled back and punched his face. Blood started
seeping from a nostril, and he swiped at it with the back of
his hand, smearing it across his cheek.

Isaac let go of the wheel, twisted around, and sprang up
on his knees. We grabbed Robert's wrists. Over and over we
told him he had a life, too; we told him the heart weakness
had been there from birth, that Timmy wasn't his fault. All
through it Robert nodded.

"Robert." Light-headed, I looked up and over to Isaac; he
wouldn't look at me.

Isaac knew, he knew too, and he'd tricked me into saying
it for him. I turned back to Robert, stuffed down there on
the car floor and told him his family had set him up and
now they were just continuing the set up, that when Timmy
died that was going to be his fault, too. He was just trying to
beat them to the punishment.

Halfway through I saw the truth was not setting Robert free. He went almost limp; he seemed to stop listening.

We both jumped when Isaac leaned on the horn and screamed. When Isaac left off screaming, he panted, "God I hate this car." He rubbed his face. "I'm ready to go home now. You want to go home?"

We looked at him. "No, I don't mean you, Al," he said deliberately, "I mean Robert. You're tired, aren't you, Robert?"

"Yeah I guess so."

"Al's got her car here. Al can take herself home. Al can do a lot of things with herself, come to think of it." Isaac's eyes were squinting at me over a razor smile.

"The same to you with mirrors," I said.

Shuffling around uneasily, Robert pulled himself back up onto the seat.

Isaac loomed over at us. "In fact if Robert would care to step out of the car, I could betray my tribal responsibilities and we could say a proper goodbye."

I liked him again then and in a minute I would like him more. "I am so sorry, Isaac," I whispered.

"God, Al. No heart. Wouldn't even consider for the sake of a sweet love lost going down on me?"

Robert popped the door and braced himself to get out. Then he said, "You don't mean that. Look at you."

Isaac sniffed deeply. He stopped Robert with a lazy hand, and then he rubbed his face again, hard. "Can you hear that? Listen." He shifted the heels of his hands around on his eyes. "Hear it? My eyes are creaking." He took his hands away and wiped them on the chest of his t-shirt. "Look, Robert," Isaac let out a breath, "this thing'll all shake down. You'll always be where you need to be. I know you will. We're all fucked anyway. Go be a rig boss. You'll be the finest."

Robert's voice trembled. "You think?"

"Fucking A."

"You really do?"

Isaac gave him one of those conclusive handshakes where

you squeeze each other's thumbs. It looked silly to me but then I saw how they locked into each other, how hard Robert was squeezing, letting himself believe.

He stomped his bare feet against the floormat then. "My legs went to sleep," he said. "Pins and needles." He laid his hands on both our shoulders and said, "I thank you, my pals." Robert slipped the gun out and just as he was going to hand it over to Isaac, gave it a twirl, western-style. Isaac grabbed, and together they mashed the trigger. The barrel must have pointed back at Robert's left hand on the door handle because in the horrible echo afterward the tips of three fingers grew red crowns.

My ears were ringing but when Isaac started to help Robert out of the car, I told him he better get his dad's gun out of here. Isaac's mouth worked soundlessly but then he got in his car and did.


WE KICKED the door open, Robert and me. I thought he could lie on the stainless steel salad table that could be washed down later, and I'd call paramedics and quit before Tottenham fired me. Streams of red ran down Robert's hand.

Tottenham glanced sideways at us, his eyes drawn by the blood spotting the floor as we struggled in but he made no move to help. He was standing with his arms out as though halting someone. The cooks were fanned out, silent and large-eyed. Vinh stood five feet away, shifting lightly from one ball of the foot to the other. Then I heard a "Get on back now, man," and saw Rupert scaling the Hobart.

Muy had Lourdes trapped in the steno chair, his hand gripping her throat. Her livid cheeks showed red marks. Tottenham was talking to him but the man did not appear to hear. He was honed in on Lourdes, intent.

"Let her go, man," Rupert murmured. He gathered both feet under him, about to jump down on the wet floor.

Muy turned his rapt face and thundered a word. His face

jutted toward us as though the word were a pinnacle or a law far beyond himself, a word so large it could never be inside himself. He meant it to reduce us all but when it did not, he turned back to Lourdes, who was tugging at his hands. Muy ripped her shirt open, then cupped his hand and slammed her across the ear. She crumpled sideways off the chair.

Rupert landed beside Muy and crowded him back just as Robert clambered over the Hobart, trailing blood. "You got him, pal?" he asked Rupert.

Rupert blocked the cook from Lourdes. "Yeah, who you?"

"Nobody," Robert said. But he knelt right down to Lourdes, got her sitting up. He fumbled with one hand, trying to button her shirt then gave up and pulled the shirt together over her small breasts. When she opened her eyes and flailed against him, he called me.

Lourdes was panting, her eyes dilated, her nostrils pinched but she clutched at me. "Rosa," she said, naming her sister. "Rosa. Es todo? No mas? Es todo?"

Yes, that's all, no more, you're safe, I told her. Before I buttoned her shirt, I caught a glimpse of the puckered dots scarred on her back and so did Robert. A shocking slickness flooded my mouth: Lourdes, in the devil's office.

Robert's voice rose. "Did he do that to her? She's so little."

The marks were old, from Buenos Aires, the silver city.

Lourdes caught sight of Robert's bloody hand then; instantly it calmed her. She seemed to know who he was. "Ah, vos tambien," she said, repeating it *you too, you too*. She wiped some blood away and assured him he would be all right. How did Robert understand that? His good hand spread wide against her back. "So little," he said.

There were loud voices as Rupert shoved the undercook out into the kitchen. Tottenham was saying Police over and over, while with desperate eyes Muy proclaimed his incomprehensible word to the Mexicans. They moved back from him. A metallic creak began to sound just as Vinh materialized offering a dampened cloth and a glass of cool water with a lemon crescent. Behind me Robert had taken the steno chair with Lourdes; she balled herself small against him. She was blowing on his bloody fingers as he inched the chair back and forth on its balky wheels, rocking her.

They made me cry. For themselves first of all, and then for the transfer ocurring between them. Robert's little infusion from Isaac had turned into tenderness for this beleaguered stranger Lourdes. Where would it go from there? I let them rock while Tottenham talked himself out of publicity—then I delivered the water with lemon. And Lourdes uncurled, focused; looking into Robert's eyes, she spit-combed his hair.

This is how, some weeks later, they come to be on the run on Xanadon. They are tired, hurt, there's a long way to go. They share a drink from a dusty canteen. They pass between them one precious smoke, Robert to Lourdes, Lourn to Rout, me to you, you back to me. In the distance, a cold dawn breaks over the mountain Kai.

Lourdes recouped her nerve. By the time the paramedics finally arrived, she leaned against the kitchen wall, smoking viciously. Robert apologized to them for taking up so much of their time.


AND THAT IS why, a few weeks later at Junie's Chuckwagon Steakhouse, I secretly and gratefully scoop from the money changer clipped to my tray enough to buy frozen margaritas for a middle-aged couple. The husband is locked into the *Houston Chronicle*, reading by the glow of a miniature lantern. The wife, in a brand new white outfit that is now ruined, her hair curled and laquered, plays wistfully with her spoon.

Me buying customers a drink? This never happens.

But on this night: I serve a draft to a sullen young man and a glass of house red to his frizzy-haired girl whose belly pooches out a pink t-shirt over a long India print skirt. The girl gives a terrified yelp, backhanding her wine glass off the table. It splashes over the middle-aged woman's white pantsuit; the woman's mouth flies open, her shocked face flames. She stands up, wine dripping down her neck into her cleavage, soaking one sleeve like artery blood.

I dash off to get a wet cloth from red-eyed Junie, who's tending bar because her husband was encouraged by their marriage counselor to defy his separation anxieties. Junie obliges sadly. "Here you go, Althea, but burgundy on white polyester is forever."

When I get back, the woman looms over the cowering girl. She takes the cloth from me, dabbing absently with one hand as the girl guides her other to the top left quadrant of her stomach. "There?" the woman asks. "You bout four, five months?"

The girl nods.

"Where's your mama? Didn't nobody tell you what to expect when?"

The girl glances wildly at the boyfriend, who scrapes back his chair and flees toward Junie and the bar. Then she forces herself back around. The girl's mouth folds first, then her face, collapsing like a tinkertoy house falling in on itself.

The woman's searching hand stops; a smile spreads across her face. "Uh huh," she says.

She sits down in the boy's chair, saying, "Turn this way, darlin." It takes some time, the woman telling and the girl listening, but the course is covered: body, time, problems, remedies, pain, milk. Their two faces, now shadowed, now glowing, draw together in the flicker of the tiny lantern.

Flushed, sweating in a leatherette cowgirl vest, I lean against the wall to stack visions in my head.


*77 EXT - FOREST IN OUTLAW TERRITORY - EVENING*
*The Stronghold base has been discovered by a Regime*

*reconnaisance patrol. The Regime's hollow-body tracers light the darkening forest. Master shot of numerous OUTLAW emplacements, the guns surplus WWXIX Lewis models. Shadows of great soaring lynwood and redbark slant across the OUTLAWS' exhausted faces. VYNN, wearing stone and feather fetish, operating tiny hand terminal, verifies coordinates for the gunners. RUPIN, cartridge belt slung across his chest, and LOURN, nicked by tracer, bandage tied around her forearm, confer.*

*A force approaches. RUPIN whirls to find I-BORK, ROUT, and the genotypes armed with small but serviceable weapons.*

*Close shot as finally RUPIN gives the barest of smiles. I-BORK distributes his troops. The fight continues as darkness falls. Then, abruptly the Regime withdraws. The tired gunners shout in celebration. RUPIN, with suspicious expression, quiets his cheering troops.*

*CUT TO:*

*78 EXT - FOREST - NIGHT*

*A grinning gunner-assistant hauls a captured Regime soldier into the clearing. LOURN rips back the hood, stares, and then brushes dirt from ALANNA's face.*

*LOURN*
*(her palm cupping ALANNA's cheek)*
*Why'd they pull out?*

*ALANNA*
*(breathless)*
*Ploy. They're waiting for reinforcements.*

*LOURN*
*How many, and when?*

*ALANNA*
*(still breathing hard)*
*Whole scad-unit packing pluton-ammo. Noon tomorrow.*

*They'll offer a truce on Convention terms but don't—*

LOURN
*(throws her head back, laughing)*
*Believe them?*

RUPIN
*(to gathering OUTLAWS)*
*Hear that? Two hour rest, then we move  out.*
*(to LIEUTENANT TOTT)*
*What's the toll?*

LIEUTENANT TOTT
*Juniz, Captain. We lost her in the first fire. And little Grego.*

A VOICE
*Yonder by the big redbark.*

RUPIN
*(pained)*
*And the . . . auxiliary troops?*
*One of the GENOTYPES points.*

CUT TO:

79 EXT - FOREST - NIGHT
*RUPIN finds ROUT holding a wounded I-BORK. ROUT (tears streaming down his striped face) chatters brokenly.*

I-BORK
*(translating, smiling faintly)*
*He says just one, Captain. His right mate I-Bork. You thought us incapable of weeping, I believe? (He lifts and turns his paw on which ROUT's tears sparkle.) When actually we are superb at it.*

*VYNN ministers to I-BORK. A rustle in the undergrowth as a*

*trembling gunner assistant, DENNISIAN, slips away. An unob-
trusive woman from the stronghold, a cook dressed in forest-stained
white, quietly shares out the tortos. The OUTLAWS eat, then sleep.
ALANNA dreams of south wind in the trees, awakens to see VYNN
dancing, his ankle bells gently tinkling. The cook, the WOMAN
IN WHITE, sits crosslegged against a great lynwood, watching.*

*From his fetish VYNN loosens a milk agate, a round, translu-
cent stone small as a pearl onion. According to the ancient texts,
it is the stone of receptiveness and attunement, facilitating the
ability to discern truth and to accept circumstances, to open. In
powdered form, it strengthens the heart and the stomach. VYNN
closes her cupped hands upon the agate and bows back from her.*

*The WOMAN IN WHITE laughs merrily and swallows the
stone. ALANNA starts—Why does this poor stupid cook not grieve
that the stronghold is lost and that those still living must flee?
Perhaps she does, her eyes glint. But look, she leans back against
her tree, brings both hands to her mouth and takes them away
overflowing with stones. These slip through her fingers, they scatter over the lyn-needles on the forest floor. She is careless with her
milky stones, profligate, with them she would cover all things.*

*No one but ALANNA sees her do this, and VYNN, but he has
known her all along. She is here, nevertheless. The OUTLAWS
sleep.*


THE WOMAN FINISHES talking, pats the girl on the back,
and returns to her table.

How can I not buy her—and her husband—margaritas? I
stick a paper parasol into the wife's and look to hand my
tray to Vinh; we both know he is the more graceful server.
But of course Vinh is not here. The husband wrenches himself from the mutual funds to ask what the drinks are for.
Can I tell him, "Sir, your wife has unbroken a piece of the
world"? "Your wife has given me joy"?

Apparently I cannot. It is a failing we spies have: our pub-
lic personae so often lack style. I look at the wife and hope

she guesses this message Rupert could have passed with a single brilliant glance. But I do not berate myself, not at all. Around midnight I will come home with my bounty, kick my fringed cowgirl skirt under the bed, and, in underwear and scuffed boots, scoot the chair to my typewriter. I will click on my old gooseneck lamp and let it burn.

# Message to
# the Nurse of Dreams

WHAT A RELIEF it would have been if Johnetta Pierce and I had met in a dream. We could have traded legs—a white set for brown, brown for white—and walked around the schoolyard in our new ones. Sawed open ribs and looked inside. Tried on each other's tongues. Traded brains and dreamed each other's dreams—all in order to answer the two questions neither of us ever asked aloud: Are you or are you not the basic same as me? Could you consider yourself my friend?

But we met in the ninth grade of Port Sabine High School. Curious as magnets, skittish, our hands fluttering from pocket to hip to lap to twirling pencil, we kept our distance and memorized each other.

I noted how Johnetta's eyebrow hairs looked like the shavings in an etch-a-sketch board, how she held herself formally, with both knees pointing in one direction and her ankles lined up, how she could hardly talk to me without breaking into an embarrassed smile, how she didn't try to hide—like the white girls—a stomach that wasn't dead flat. I don't know what she recorded about me. But early on I caught her calcu-

lating if I was human in the same way she was. I swear. That's
what made me like her—that she'd do that. Johnetta studied
me, puzzled, trying to determine what sort of shape flickered inside me and measure it against her own. That was the
kind of logical, common sense activity I understood.

One bothered day I trudged over to the bus bench where
we had first started talking. We knew each other by then.
Johnetta had her pencil out, drawing on notebook paper.
Not taking her eyes from the paper, she still scooted over for
me, a downward smile curling her lips, though I had plenty
of room to sit. I sat, and let fall a remark about the girls at
our school. From my point of view it was an objective, socio-
logical remark about these girls saying things they did not
mean which was somehow not supposed to be lying but just
a clever language they spoke. Johnetta heard me. But she
seemed so calm, so intent on her drawing that it was like
talking to someone sewing, someone listening and not listening. That incited me. I said I'd dreamed those girls were
candles, the plain kind you rummage around for when a hurricane has blown down the electricity. And one by one I
tipped a match to their flat wax heads.

I wanted her to sympathize with me but I was also seized
by a conflicting urge to see what she was drawing.

Johnetta moved her pencil sideways, shading. She asked,
"What they done to you?" which made me feel a momen-
tary backlash against her for getting straight to a point I
wanted to complain to the left or right of. So I had to admit
I overheard two girls in the lunch line talking about a swimming party and when they saw I was listening, they said oh
I should come too. But when I went to their house on Saturday they'd already gone. I had to get back in the car with my
mother and my dry bathing suit rolled up in my dry towel
and go back home.

I kicked the bench but that knocked Johnetta's hand off
the paper so I stopped. By craning I saw her drawing was
dark people flying up with their feet off the ground. They

looked like dead people taking off for heaven. Their palms were out and their faces tilted casually skyward. It looked like they'd bounced off a trampoline and were just heading on up.

"What is that?" I asked her.

"Dream I had last night," she said, sketching the short ends of a girl's hair streaming out.

"What was it about?" I said.

But Johnetta distracted me with, "So they ast you to come to that party."

"Yeah," I said, grievance churning my stomach again.

"And you thought they meant it, huh?"

She raised her head then. Her sparse eyebrows lifted. That direct look shut me right up but it also did this—it slid the worst onus back on those girls. As for me, I could see in her eyes she was saying *You got a lot to learn, don't you?* though no such message came out of her mouth. The essential thing about Johnetta and me was that we had one essential thing— we heard things without actually hearing them. When her bus rolled up hissing its brakes, she folded her drawing into her pencil bag and stood up. "That wasn't no true dream, was it?" she asked with her embarrassed smile, about the girls being utility candles. Because I begrudged her the smoothness of knowing that I lied, "Yeah it was."

Johnetta climbed on the bus. And then I couldn't bear the lie because lying was not within the boundaries we had established, at least so far as I knew. I ran down the sidewalk until I got even with her bus seat. "It was a true *day*dream," I yelled at her. I felt relieved then, telling her the truth. In those days I badly needed to be straight with somebody, even somebody who never used my name back to me like I used hers. Johnetta mashed her face against the window making me laugh until an old black lady beside her jerked her hair back sternly. No old white lady would have done that to me. "Old people," she'd told me once, and in such a way that I knew she didn't consider this necessarily bad, "they mind everbody's business."

"Hey," I asked, the next time I sat with her, "what were those flying-up people? That one in the middle with her hair blowing—she looked like you."

Johnetta's eyes lit with a shy and secret gleam.

Now it seems to me that what Johnetta Pierce and me did mostly and best was ask each other questions. We were fourteen years old, we didn't know anything. But we were trying; such was the basis of our short and peculiar association.

I LEFT PORT SABINE, Texas, more than twenty years ago, so the last time I saw her must have been around 1970 or 1971, a couple of years after we graduated. I was at a carwash killing time. When I'd got tired of making rainbows with the carwash water, I pulled the car over in the corner, sat down out of the way, and read my library book. After maybe ten pages, a shadow blocked my light and I glanced up into the September glare. Broad planks of sunlight shined out around a body. Took a minute to get her into focus—a dark, down-peering face with sweat diamonds in the wispy hair. "Johnetta, is that you?" I asked.

She was wearing shorts and some laceless tennies with the heels walked on and had a grocery sack clamped in her arms. "What you doin at this place?" she asked me back.

I pointed toward my husband Danny's car. Dried water streaks had painted it in a faint stalagtite pattern.

She lifted an eyebrow. She always did have the nimblest eyebrows, which if you cared to observe, and I had cared to observe, would wing around on her face. "What is it you think you done to that car?"

"My duty."

The eyebrows arched.

"When he got drafted, my husband said to maintain his vehicle."

She pulled her head back on her neck. "You went and got

*168*

yourself married?"

I held up my gold band.

She snorted. "What's wrong with your mind you didn't get no rock, girl?"

"Johnetta, how you doing?" I asked her.

We smiled at each other then. She hadn't used my name and I thought maybe she didn't remember it. We hadn't had much contact since the ninth grade when Port Sabine High finally integrated, the year we tried to be friends. But she'd never used my name then, either. I'd realized that was particular to Johnetta's private rules of intimacy, which I'd respected but could not divine.

She ended the smile by gazing over her shoulder. "How I'm doin? House caught fire and burnt up everything we had." She shifted the grocery sack so she could pluck at her faded Houston Astros t-shirt. "Neighbors give me this nice clothes."

I flashed on my daydream of melting the girls' heads. That seemed a long, silly time ago. We were into real time now. "God. Anybody get hurt?"

"Got scared." She hugged the sack, still looking far over her shoulder.

"Johnetta, are you really okay?"

She turned and nodded but at the same moment stepped back. I'd hit her too-deep-too-soon marker so I waded back to shallow water with a question. "Not married yet?"

"Sweet Jesus and hell no. I am a young thing."

She asked me was my husband supporting me in style. I could see Johnetta had money on the brain as who wouldn't who all they owned was a second-hand Houston Astros t-shirt and a grocery sack. But I had to disappoint her. I told her I had a job at the Credit Bureau. Then I described our garage apartment behind an old brick duplex. I added that my husband Danny was due home from basic in about three hours. Danny had told me on the phone that the *second* thing he meant to do after he got in the door was take off his army boots but I did not mention this. It had no place in our conversation, which was a shame.

She told me she worked at a dry cleaners. "That chemicals they use, I wake up with my eyes swole and a ache right here . . ." She pinched the skin between her eyebrows.

When she took her hand off the groceries to do that, a corner of a milk carton poked through the dampened sack. "Lord," Johnetta laughed, grabbing it. She'd lost the stiff posture of ninth grade; she looked tired but easier in her body. A jealous pinch told me I'd gone the other way; I was restless and full of desires.

"You look different," I told her.

"Girl," she said, all wishing-voiced and faraway, "I would be if I could. I would let somebody run they big old Cadillac right into my mama's rattletrap Ford and collect a pile of insurance money." She hummed, holding her groceries together. Then she caught sight of the library book I was reading, splayed out on the pavement by my knee.

Johnetta's face became sly. Behind the slyness lurked a genuine shyness and her eyes shone like I remembered. She asked, "What you want to read that book for?"

With a start, I realized: I am reading it because you and I didn't stay friends. If we had I might not have picked this book though I would still like reading it.

For about three seconds it was as strong as it ever was, a place that lived between us that we could both go into. "Because this is a powerful book," I said. "You want a ride to wherever you live now?"


I HAD BEEN finishing up *Manchild in the Promised Land*. It seems strange to think I was using a big-city black boy with a life far harder than mine as a model but I surely was. I was holed up in the concrete corner of a carwash wondering where I could find half the nerve Claude Brown had. I'd gone back to read one of the folded-down pages. It was the part where Claude Brown's father shows him the shell game, and he never picks the shell with the pea under it. Ten times he picks the wrong shell. His daddy has the pea in his hand all along, and he warns his son that's what he's going to spend his life doing, looking for a pea that isn't there. He's telling his boy not to be a fool. But fools can be the most practical, self-interested people there are. They are disgusted by the press and clutter of fear. Either they get the great relief of a clean heart or they die, so they will keep on. Claude Brown keeps looking the whole book, he does the hardest looking I'd ever heard about. In the end it's like he has to make a whole new pea since he can't find one where it should have been.


JOHNETTA WAS STAYING at her cousin's apartment in Seventh Heaven. That was a block of apartments put up by a white contractor and painted the colors he imagined black people favored: pink, green, lemon meringue yellow, and blue. We had to walk up some stairs without a railing—just steps rising in the air—and Johnetta said that's why her mama wasn't staying there, those stairs.

The sack had busted; I followed her up carrying the milk and a big jar of Maxwell House Instant. She knocked on the pink door, pulled out a key and opened it in her cousin's face.

He was tall, with wirerim glasses and a medium Afro. At the hem of his navy blue bathrobe were knees that ran into skinny shins just like Johnetta's. He blinked at me. Then he looked at Johnetta and as we went past, she told him we used to know each other in high school. I said Hi and my name. "Walter," he said back. Glancing around, I saw the furniture in here looked like Danny's and mine, stuff the relatives didn't want. A sneeze would scatter the spindly-legged dinette and the olive green couch would fold out, like our yellow and brown plaid one with sprung buttons. No AC but a big square fan near a raised window.

Johnetta loaded the refrigerator. I passed her the milk and set the coffee on the gold-flecked kitchen counter. Then I stood there feeling light-handed and extra.

"Walter just started law school," Johnetta said, over her shoulder.

"Yeah? Neat." I gave him a smile, partly nervous and partly curious and admiring. I had recently developed a yearning to go to college myself.

Walter returned the smile like he was used to that response. "Go on, have a seat," he said. "Your hair's nice."

My hair touched the small of my back; it was dark and straight, wet at the neck from the heat outside. "Thank you. Is law school hard?"

Walter had sat down in an elderly armchair next to a pile of books. At my question, his shoulders drew in protectively. But he said, "Not really. Done Contracts and Criminal Law this morning. Got a class tonight in Civil Procedure." He hefted a big slick book from the floor and weighted his lap with it. I sat on the olive green couch, the backs of my knees riding on the metal frame beneath the cushions. I imagined Johnetta hauling this heavy sucker open every night; mornings, stuffing it shut, tangled sheets and all.

She came in, squatted in front of the fan, and let it blow on her. She had her head tilted back just like the flying-up people in her dream; the tips of her hair spiked out. A chill rippled the sweat on my backbone, but I turned to her cousin and asked him what kind of law he intended to practice.

"Here be the black Perry Mason," Johnetta said.

"You shut up, Johnetta." Walter tugged on his lapels, drawing the robe together at the neck.

For some reason her teasing killed our baby conversation. I was about to stand up to go when Walter said, "Scuse me, will ya'll?" and fled into the bedroom, closing the door.

I thought he was going to get dressed but Johnetta's eyes narrowed. "You smoke dope?"

"Danny does. Makes me woozy."

"You be glad when he get home, huh?"

"Sure," I said.

For a second she concentrated on me; I didn't feel like looking back at her. Then we just sat there smelling pot and finally Johnetta scrambled up and banged the door, calling, "You know you got your school in three hours, Walter."

The door banged back once.

She threw herself down by the fan again. Its *rrrrr* was the only sound.

"Hey," I said after a while, and asked her if she'd had any dreams lately. Her face cleared. She smiled and kicked off the walked-on sneakers. "Lord you member how we used to do?"

YES I DID. I did remember. I had to take the city bus on Fridays and Johnetta often did, and one Friday 13th she was out on the bench alone so I sat down beside her. A sunny autumn day with the sweetgums and the sycamores casting yellow leaves at us. The bus was late. Hi, I said and my name and she said hers back. We looked at each other, shyly, and it seemed like she was appraising me, trying to figure me out, but in a welcome way. I must have been taking her in, too. In my mind I said, *What is it like being at this new school with all these strange white kids, is it like hard work?* and in her mind she said back, *Yes, it is a whole lotta work and I would rather be in my neighborhood, easy with my real friends* and to that I admitted *I don't have any friends, I just moved to this school and I hate the way these kids are* and she sympathized, *Yeah it sure is hard going to a new place* and that was generous coming from her because the change she'd made was greater than mine. Out loud, though, I said only what was bothering me that day, that the night before I'd had a bad dream. Now this wasn't the most unpersonal subject to bring up, like the weather or school, and that's when Johnetta gave me her determining look. I found myself holding still as if for a verdict, as if whatever she saw would matter to me.

A light came into her eyes so I let out my breath and told her the dream. "Here it is," I said. "I was lying in bed next to a window screen. It was dark. A man with silver hair turned into the driveway on a motorcyle and rode up without making a sound. His motorcycle glided to my window. He had on a red shirt and a white tie and he just peered in the window at me for the longest time. He kept whispering something I couldn't hear."

Johnetta didn't laugh. She saw I was upset, plus she believed in dreams.

"Watch yourself," she said. "Something fixin to happen. That man is announcin it to you." Her face mirrored my own intent expression. I wanted to scoot over on the bench and lock my arm with hers. But I didn't.

"My aunt used to get one," Johnetta offered right back to me, "that when it came something bad always gon happen. And all it was was the color white. She'd be walkin along somewheres and there be a woman in a white party dress. Or a hat with a white bird feather. One time she dream of a long white car and she wake up cryin and sure enough the next week her daddy grab his chest and fall over dead."

My mouth dropped open. We inched nearer each other. Clear burning daylight and we sat there at the bus stop with our eyes bugged out.

We liked scaring each other because we could jump right in that scared place together. It was just our particular natural ground, that fun, shivery place. It let us go on to how often dreams worked like messages (we thought *Always* if you could only decipher the message) and were our lives set, every day engraved on a tablet in a vault somewhere like the First National Heavenly Bank (this seemed *Pointless* to us), or could we change them around (we thought *Yes* if you were persistent and bold).

Johnetta's method for deciphering dreams required that first we quiz each other in order to determine what feeling accompanied the dream. Was it frightening and ominous, a heavy sinking in the chest like a dragweight? Or was it a hopeful opening that made you rise up to meet it, there in the bed? Once we had that, we tried out various interpretations of the dream. If we could hit on the correct message, the feeling came back as reliably as a note of piano music, as though we'd finally struck two fingers on the right eerie key.

Now we had to reveal some private things in order to get at these dreams properly. Like she knew about the neighbors calling the cops on one of my parents' fights and I knew about her sister that died so young before she could really get started living. Once Johnetta confided she might like to be a nurse, did they have nurses of dreams? She laughed to cover up her seriousness. Both of us understood that that information stayed right where it was, on our bus bench. I thought sometime I would get bold enough to ask her to go home with me so we could keep on talking but that never happened. She never invited me, either. Her bus pulled up, and I said "Bye, Johnetta" and she said plain "Bye" and for me Friday was over and done with.

Next year a federal judge ordered old G.W. Carver closed for good, so loads more black kids enrolled in the tenth grade. Johnetta hooked up with some girls she'd known before. Once I went and stood with her, when she was surrounded by her old friends. They smiled at me and said Hi but all the loud joking about C-cups and double D's simmered down. "You lettin your hair grow," Johnetta noticed and I complimented a womanish straight skirt I hadn't seen her wear before. We spoke like we were in the back pew at a funeral home. I knew, somehow, that she wouldn't appreciate me dragging up any dreams around those girls. After that we just said Hi when we passed in the halls. Every once in a while at my locker somebody would punch me and I'd turn around to see Johnetta going by.

JOHNETTA SAID, "No, I hadn't had me much dreams lately,

cept about the fire. Sometimes there just a bunch a smoke and I can't see nothing clear." She shrugged, like she was sorry she didn't have more but that was just how it was now. I was ready for that answer. We weren't fourteen anymore; we had jobs to worry about and men. Social life ranked after all that. But a mild sadness sounded in my heart anyway.

"You havin any?" she asked.

I could have told her a dream about Danny but it wasn't really frightening, it just made me feel guilty and besides, Walter returned then, all loose-shouldered. He got a six-pack of malt liquor tallboys out of the icebox. The cans had chess horses on them. We, at least Walter and me, poured them down while Johnetta said she'd heard from somebody that one of our old teachers had been arrested for DWI. So we started one of those fallback conversations. I asked her if she remembered Jimmy Cooley, who used to raise the flag every day. She shook her head, and I told her he'd drowned last year fishing. And that Ted Dupuis went up to Huntsville, serving 5 to 10.

"What he done? I remember that boy's nasty mouth."

"Forging checks, robbing stuff, stole his father's car and broke his arm."

"Beat his own daddy?" Johnetta recoiled. "That is an evil son. You member Tevis Johnson?"

"Big guy with a round head and wrinkled forehead? I think he was in my math class. The one the coach taught." I squinted. "Was he the one they wanted him to play football and he told them—"

"Yeah, yeah," Johnetta was nodding, "his mama had definite ideas. Tevis tell that coach, 'My mama says I ain't go play no football, I'm gon play math.'"

I sat up and pointed. "He said that in my class!"

Her nod turned sad. "He down at the VA now. Got his right leg blowed off at the knee. Right eye messed up too, but you know he still have a plan. He's figurin to—" She was going to go on, I could tell, we were moving into a conversation women might have, between themselves. I didn't believe it would get off the ground with Walter there but I was so keen on plans I leaned forward anyway, to hear about Tevis's. Sure enough Walter interrupted.

"Johnetta carry herself down the VA," Walter swallowed a big swallow of malt liquor and wiped his mouth, "ever Saturday morning."

"So what?" Johnetta barked but Walter waved her off, smiling to himself, not wanting a fight.

". . . just that," he started laughing, "the last time he was complainin cause they give him a white leg. As a temporary till the black legs come in."

At first I didn't laugh but then I did because Walter had such a merry laugh it got me going. I sputtered some beer, and Johnetta finally joined in. The malt liquor was spangling us out fast.

Johnetta's fine smile got complicated when she looked at Walter. "Show her how you gon do," she urged, "when you take that bar."

Walter's mouth hiked up on one side and his eyes cut toward her but he did not move.

I popped another tallboy, sank into the couch, and let my body drift into a wide slow space. "C'mon, Walter," I said. "C'mon c'mon c'mon." I expected an accomplished oration with habeas corpuses and flagrante delictos in it.

Walter took another long swallow and uncrossed his legs. "Okay. Y'all want do criminal?"

"Yeah!" Johnetta perked up.

"Then who got themself murdered?"

"Landlord," she sipped from her beer.

"Could be," Walter pursed his lips, "or could be that raisinhead Contracts teacher with his long pointin finger."

They looked at me. "I don't know," I said, "the President?"

Walter rolled his eyes.

"Miss America?"

Johnetta laughed at that one.

Walter waved his hands back and forth. "Now you got to understand they wouldn't hire me for that," he said. "They hire old F. Lee. You got to be real now."

Walter, it struck me, would dig his garden better than most. But he would not go so far as to create a whole new pea. He was not like Claude Brown, he was not that kind of fool.

"Understand what I'm sayin?" Walter massaged his temples. "You got to get closer to home here."

Okay, closer to home. It slipped out. "My husband Danny?" I said.

Johnetta's eyes became all lid. She said, "You messin with it"; she did not say what I was messing with. It seemed as if she might ask me something but she kept quiet.

Walter stood up rubbing his hands together and pointed to Johnetta. She knew exactly what to do: sat in the armchair and slapped the air. "Johnetta S. Pierce and I swear to tell the truth, the whole truth and nothing but the truth so help me God," she said.

"What is your profession, Miss Pierce?"

"I don't know but not what it is right now." She held her right hand up again. That was an oath, too. So I saw how wrong I'd been before—Johnetta harbored some restless desires herself. I caught her eye then. *You wanted to be a nurse* was in my mind and she read it, she always could. She looked away from me as if I might embarrass her with what she'd said in private when we were kids waiting for a bus.

Walter frowned at her answer but only briefly. "Tell the court what you saw on the night in question, Miss Pierce."

"What?"

He had to repeat the question.

Johnetta shook herself and answered solemnly. "Soldier boy layin on the groun with a hole shot through him."

"Regrettable," Walter murmured. "What else did you see?"

"Saw her with a big old gun."

"Hey," I protested, surprised, "no fair."

Walter gestured for silence. "Was she pointing that big old gun at the victim?"

Johnetta started to answer then stopped. "You leadin the witness."

"Damn, just—" But he changed his question. "What did you see her do with the gun?"

"You better be sure of that identification," I warned her. My feelings stung. I did regret blurting out Danny's name. I wanted him and me to be just fine, and Johnetta and me to be together against somebody else, and me not to have such a big mouth.

Walter turned on me. "Court cautions the spectators to be quiet or the bailiff gon remove they ass," he said. He swiveled back to Johnetta. "What did you see her do with the gun, Miss Pierce?"

"Oh baby," she sighed, staring at me, her eyes remorseless and amused and not judging at all. "That gun? She raise the barrel of it to her mouth and blow."

My forehead went hot. We just kept looking at each other. We were together against something, though what it was was hazy, whatever it is that keeps you from being what you need to be.

"Witness may step down. Court calls the wife of the so recently deceased."

"Wait a minute," I said. "Are you the defense or the prosecution?" I just meant I was confused as to their rules.

Johnetta spoke right up for him. "Walter got to hit em anyway they come."

Walter blotted his neck and upper lip with his bathrobe sleeve and motioned to me. So I went and sat in the armchair.

"State your full legal name for the court."

"Mrs. Daniel J. Kelly."

"State your profession, Mrs. Kelly."

"I am a skip-tracer for the Credit Bureau."

"Say what?" Walter paused; Johnetta's eyebrows winged

up.

"A skip-tracer. I locate people who ran off without paying their bills. Then the collectors go after them."

"That's some bad job," Walter commented, just as Walter; he wasn't telling me anything I didn't know. He reverted to his lawyer demeanor. "Very well, Mrs. Kelly. You are married. Were married. What kind of a man was your late husband?"

"Regular," I said. "Mostly nice but sometimes not."

"I see. And how would you describe your feelings for Mr. Daniel J. Kelly?"

I thought about all those letters from camp in Danny's choked handwriting. About the time he got me to smoke with him and then we made love until we fell out of bed on the floor and still kept going. I thought about when I told him I wanted to go to college and Danny said not on his dime.

"I guess they would be regular, too."

"Regular. Um hmm. Will you tell the court where you were on the aforementioned evening?"

"I was at the apartment of . . ." I started to say friends but I was too chicken to presume, that's the sorrow of the whole thing, somebody's got to presume. What I said was ". . . Johnetta Pierce and her cousin Walter."

"I see. Is it true your husband carried a substantial insurance policy?"

I pretended to pull on the fingertips of white cotton gloves. Johnetta snickered and Walter smiled. It seemed like I was doing something right so I went along with his question. "Why yes," I said, "he did take out a policy."

"And what might be the amount of that policy?"

I said the biggest amount we could imagine back then. "One million dollars."

"One mil-lion dollars." Walter withdrew knowingly.

The fan whirred. It was baking in that apartment. Walter strolled around; in no hurry, he flicked a speck from his sleeve.

"This case plain as daylight," Johnetta burst out, "got a eye witness, motive—"

"The court will tolerate no disorder," Walter reprimanded her. "Nobody ast you nothing."

Before she had time to bristle at him, Walter whipped off his wirerims, whirled and pointed them at me. I glanced toward the slit in the bathrobe. It didn't go up far enough but he saw me look. He leaned over, smack in my face, he set his hands on the arms of the chair.

Like that, Walter's maleness reached in and my femaleness rushed up and we almost shuddered in the collision.

Without the opaque glasses, Walter's face was unobstructed and beautiful. His face looked like a far, wide plain whose breezes are mild. I saw he could master this lawyer routine but he would have to adjust himself all the time to keep straight with that life. I knew how that felt; you adjust and adjust and one day soon you are set like concrete in a form you never meant to take.

"I put it to you," Walter breathed in my face, "that you were not at that apartment on the fateful night. I put it to you that you were at your own domicile, with a gun waiting for your husband to come home. Isn't that the truth, Mrs. Kelly?"

"That's a lie," I said. That thought dried my tongue; I tilted and drained the chess horse can. Danny and I might not always get along but I wouldn't hurt him. In fact a lot of the time I was washing his car I had been thinking how crummy a thing it would be to hurt Danny.

"A lie? The prosecution believes it is no lie. You planned this cold-blooded crime, you executed it without pity, and now you are perjuring yourself to this court!" Walter was thundering, he made me shrink down in the witness armchair. "You are lying, Mrs. Kelly, lying to save your own—"

Johnetta interjected, "You badgerin her, Walter."

Walter jerked around. "Godamnit, will you just let me do this my ownself?"

"But that's what that book says, says badgerin the witness is when—"

"How come you readin my book? That's my book."

"Why I can't read your damn book—"

"Mr. Dry Cleaner asking your legal advice?"

Johnetta's mouth drew into an ugly knot. I stuck my hand up, wanting to stop this. "Look," I said, "I put it that I didn't kill anybody. And Miss Pierce didn't kill anybody—" The murder here had been committed by my heart, the way it does, independently—kills someone off or preserves them long after they are gone from your life. But I could not bear to see that yet. So I was about to say, I put it to you that in an hour or so my husband Danny is going to come walking up to our domicile just as alive as you or me.

Walter didn't give me the chance. He clutched his hands behind his back and paced away from the witness chair. Under the bathrobe, his bunched shoulders stretched and strained. He muttered, "Can't nobody just be but they got to mess with somebody else when they should be studyin their own case . . ." Johnetta's chin shot out. Walter ducked his head and pivoted away from her, toward me again.

With Johnetta quiet, he honed in. His gentle face hardened and, to match, his voice slid into a sarcastic tone—he'd practiced this style before. "Now. Mrs. Kelly. What really occurred on that tragic night?"

I was wishing I knew how it worked when it was just them together, him and Johnetta. But that was not the essential point. Now I know that I could have broken down and confessed on the stand, I could have shouted the name of the real murderer, I could have concocted a whole new angle. A whole new pea. But I didn't.

"Come now, Mrs. Kelly. Why else are we assembled here today? If not for the truth?"

The truth? What are we doing here? Stupidly, all I could think was, The truth is I came to see Johnetta and to talk to her like we used to talk.

I turned toward her. Her fingers were laced; idly she crossed one thumb over the other. "So what's the answer, counselor?" she asked him. Before he'd had any real time to respond, she crossed thumbs again and went on, "I thought you said lawyers wasn't never supposed to ask a question they didn't know the answer to."

Walter looked harassed. He went back in the bedroom again and came out with his roach lit. He sank onto the floor, slid the round specs over his eyes, and sucked smoke. Johnetta stuck her watch dial under his nose. "You promised everbody you was letting that shit alone on school days. I heard you." She kicked his bare foot.

Walter's hand just floated up and closed over her wrist. "Johnetta . . ." He began a soft plea, with that patience pot gives you. He was about to say something she needed to hear so I muttered, "I gotta go now," and waved but Walter didn't see.

The fight had gone out of Johnetta's shoulders. Murmuring, "Just a minute," she extricated her wrist. She shut the pink door and walked me halfway down the railless steps. We couldn't find anything to say and finally I said, "Well maybe I will run into you at the dry cleaners," and she said "Shit." That seemed to give her some relief. She seemed freed up enough then to ask me a couple of questions. I answered the last one without speaking a word and we went our separate ways.


I WAS NAKED in the door when Danny showed up. I was playing the radio. Danny came trotting down the driveway to our tiny back house, all army green and sunburn, his nose peeling. He let out a whoop, the duffle bumped his back. He ran through the shadow of the shade tree and out into the sunlight. That's how I remember him, lit up in the last mellow burst before the day faded, thinking it was all for him. But I'd been naked since I got home from Johnetta and

Walter's. That was my relief. I'd raided Danny's stash and thrown off my clothes, dancing on tiptoe, raising my arms high, turning this way and that. The sun beamed me its invisible gold, the September air passed powerfully through my skin. I was sifting from this body. I was feeling nothing between what was most essentially me and every other piece of nature in this bright dark world.

THESE WERE THE two questions Johnetta Pierce asked me right before I never saw her again. "Say you find people that run off and left all their bills?"

"Yep." We were halfway down or halfway up those airy stairsteps I couldn't figure which.

"You come across my name owing a bunch of bills, would you find me?"

It would be nice to describe how I hugged her shoulder then but I didn't. I was sort of pissed that she acted like that's all she wanted of me. Nice to report that at this fitting juncture she finally said my name but she didn't. She didn't ever call my name. But she did give me that sly-shy smile, the one we started out with back in ninth grade, that tender question mark.

So that's all you want to know—Would I send bill collectors after you? My head shook No and as oath my index finger cut an X across my heart.

But we both knew you asked more than that, and I answered more. You still say, in my mind, *Is there any place you would find me?* and I answer without a word, still tapping the index finger on my heart. That's all my message is, and it is going out to you, Johnetta, wherever you are.

**Lisa Sandlin** was born in Beaumont, Texas and has one son, Evan. She received her bachelor of arts from Rice University and her master of fine arts from Vermont College. In 1995 she was the recipient of the Dobie-Paisano Fellowship awarded jointly by the Texas Institute of Letters and The University of Texas at Austin; in the previous year she received a fellowship from the National Endowment for the Arts. She currently teaches fiction writing at Wayne State in Nebraska. Her first collection of short stories, *The Famous Thing About Death*, was published by Cinco Puntos Press in 1991.

We've been publishing books by Texas women for years now, but in a flash of genius we saw how completely unique, vibrant, and in-your-face their collective writing is. Like Texas. Hell yes! So we started a series.

To date the Hell Yes! Texas Women's Series includes:

***Message to the Nurse of Dreams,*** by Lisa Sandlin.
ISBN 0-938317-27-X/Paper/192 pages/$11.95.

***Keepers of the Earth,*** by LaVerne Harrell Clark.
ISBN 0-938317-28-8/Paper/356 pages/$14.95.

***In Search of the Holy Mother of Jobs***, by Pat LittleDog.
ISBN 0-938317-15-6/Paper/128 pages/$9.95.

***The Famous Thing About Death***, by Lisa Sandlin.
ISBN 0-938317-13-X/Paper/128 pages/$9.95.

***Sonahchi, A Collection of Myth Tales***, by Pat Carr.
ISBN 0-938317-06-7/Paper/80 pages/$8.95.

For further information, or a catalog of all Cinco Puntos Press titles, please call 1-800-566-9072, or write us at 2709 Louisville, El Paso, TX 79930.